The Chestnut Roaster

Also by Eve McDonnell

Elsetime

Praise for *The Chestnut Roaster*

'Eve has done it again! Like reading a poem: beautiful, mysterious and captivating.'

Kieran Larwood, author of the *Five Realms Series*

'Beautiful, dreamily-strange adventure tale for readers 9+.'

Claire Hennessy, author of *Like Other Girls*

'Eve McDonnell has created a wonderful world full of invention and mystery. This is a thrilling fantasy that will sweep you off your feet!'

Patricia Forde, author of *The Wordsmith*

'Just phenomenal! I went overland and underland & every space in between through the city of light and dark, loving every step MAGNIFIQUE! 'What matters is inside, I promise.' True magic.'

Zillah Bethell, author of *The Shark Caller*

'The depths of Eve McDonnell's imagination are astounding. An immersive, sensory, exciting journey through Paris in the year 1888. An exciting, fast-paced, whirlwind of a story.'

Sinéad O'Hart, author of *The Eye of the North*

Praise for *Elsetime*

'Fans of Helena Duggan will love the atmosphere and clever plotting. A highly original debut.'

Irish Independent

'Rich with historical detail – *Elsetime* is both classic in tone and original in vision.'   *Irish Times*

'The characters are splendidly drawn. A remarkable debut which features a brilliant and surprising ending'

Irish Examiner

'The plot swirls and sparkles and will keep readers on tenterhooks.'

LoveReading4Kids Debut of the Month

'Steeped in atmosphere and suspense, beautifully written. *Elsetime* is gripping, moving, and delivers a final, dazzling twist that will delight readers both young & old.'   *Lancashire Post*

'An enchanting, time twisting adventure. Beautifully written.'   *Kieran Larwood*

'Eve McDonnell's gripping story weaves delicately through time, with a brilliant twist in the tale that will leave you longing for Glory and Needles' next adventure!' *Helena Duggan*

'Written in a unique and memorable voice, and peopled with characters as memorable as the wonderful Needle and the spirited Glory, Eve McDonnell's debut novel is one not to miss.'

Sinéad O'Hart

'Glorious storytelling indeed.' *Nicki Thornton*

'A tale that combines time-travel with evocative description, colourful characterisation and artistic endeavour to create a unique and compelling story of friendship and courage.' *Steve Voake*

~ SHORTLISTED FOR THE
SPELLBINDING BOOK AWARD 2021 ~

~ SHORTLISTED FOR THE
AWESOME BOOK AWARD 2022 ~

~ WINNER, CHILDREN'S BOOK AWARD
(pre publication) WELLS FESTIVAL OF
LITERATURE 2017 ~

The Chestnut Roaster

Eve McDonnell

Internal illustrations by Ewa Beniak-Haremska

Published in the UK by Everything with Words Limited
Fifth Floor, 30–31 Furnival Street, London EC4A 1JQ

www.everythingwithwords.com

A catalogue record of this book is available
from the British Library.

ISBN   978–1–911427–29–2

Printed and bound in Great Britain by
CPI Group (UK) Ltd, Croydon CR0 4YY

Eve McDonnell wishes to thank the Arts Council for the
bursary that allowed her to research and write this book.

What matters is
Inside, I promise.
Tucked; a seed of life, a shining star,
And the gloss of a giant.
I promise, inside
Is what matters.

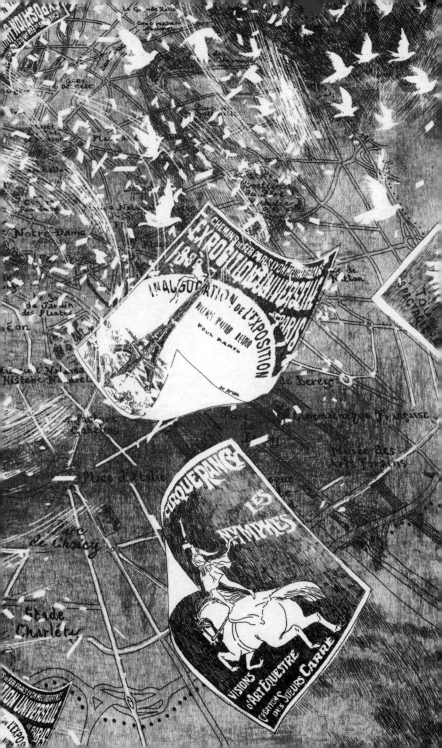

For Dad

Overground

On her corner, where the quiet Rue du Dragon meets
the bustling Boulevard Saint-Germain, petite Piaf Durand
– a girl who cannot forget, even if she wanted to –
stands at her chestnut roaster.

A stranger arrives.

One | Un

Piaf's Corner, Rue du Dragon, Paris

The smell of roasting chestnuts clouded around her, hug-like; the kind of smell that flared nostrils and clamped eyes shut, but Piaf did not blink. The stranger leaned closer, so close the dangling gold button on his coat tipped the pyramid of chestnuts between them. The top chestnut rolled onto the roasting cart's hot pan, and hissed. Piaf let it be.

"Of course you remember me, girl!" the stranger said, all smarmy and sweet as macarons. He leaned against Piaf's roasting cart until its old wheels screeched in disapproval. "We met when you were younger – on your seventh birthday. I brought you a puppet."

Piaf chewed her lip, fidgeted. What an odd thing to say. The man didn't look like a liar, all dressed up like that with his smile and serious coat. She stared down at the pyramid's fallen chestnut. Had there been a full moon last night? Every visitor to the roaster that morning had a madness about them. For once, they did not speak of the treasure stolen from Notre-Dame. The small Cabinet of Oils and its mysterious powers had been shrouded in so much curiosity that talk of its disappearance had dripped from tips of tongues in her roaster's queue for the guts of a long year. Not so today. Instead, regular customers and strangers alike were searching pockets for coins they were sure were there, losing things, finding things, non-stop gasping and talking nonsense. But *this* stranger was different. He was a liar.

"I do not remember you. I am sorry, Monsieur," said Piaf. She'd dug deep for manners. "Will it be just the one cone of chestnuts, or two?"

"I'm a cousin," the stranger insisted, "to your mother." While a finger of black smoke rose like a crooked branch from the burning chestnut between

4

them, he mapped out an imaginary family tree in the air above her head. She studied the man's skin – grey with pores clogged with oily sweat. A dead fish sprung to mind. He shook the thin wrist of the girl he held at arm's length but did not release his grip. "So, I believe that makes you two cousins, too," he said. Piaf stared at the girl and took note: her eyelids were heavy, sore looking, and she breathed through her mouth. Now that the morning's fog had finally sunk down to the ground like a thick layer of vanilla cream, the low October sun was free to cast a crooked shadow across her face.

What happened to your nose? Piaf wanted to ask. There was this one time when the back of her twin brother's head gave her the best nosebleed in all of Paris... Piaf's memory niggled to tell the story, but she quickly pulled her hand up her coat sleeve and twisted her secret button until it felt tight between her fingers. The button, with its three tiny squirrels curled together in a circle, was carved from wood and sewn onto the inside of her cuff. It mightn't have been gold and heavy like the stranger's, but to Piaf it was worth more than his – for starters, it was a Pufont's Button Bijouterie original. But, best of all, it could stop her non-stop, nagging memory dead – even when incessant fidgeting failed to do the job. It was just a silly distraction according to Luc, telling her she'd have to sell one hundred chestnuts to buy just one, but whatever her twin brother thought, twisting it kept her here – *in the now.*

Piaf let the button go. Before it had even unspun, the urge to fidget returned, every twitch of muscle fighting the lure of her memory. Fearing she'd get lost in the endless maze of tunnels inside her mind, she scratched at her cheeks and she tapped her toes and twitched as though an ant crawled across her skin.

The man hissed at her movements, and Piaf noticed the slight swatting of his hand. She annoyed him, she was a horsefly.

She focused on the girl. Her heavy-lidded eyes now latched on hard – proper eye contact; no flicking up and down or raising an eyebrow. Neither Piaf's fidgeting nor her small height seemed to bother the girl, not even a bit.

Piaf gasped when the man spoke again:

"SO, COME, dear child! Come along with us, this minute. A storm is predicted, and your mother insists you take shelter with us." He smiled, but the twist

6

in his jaw and shift of his top hat told Piaf he was grinding his teeth.

Piaf looked up. The sky was blue, not a cloud in sight. "I said I do not remember you." Piaf's words were louder this time, and blunt – each syllable exaggerated by her fidgeting. Just as she had intended.

The man turned his head to one side, his stare stronger through one eye. "Your brother needs your mother's care today. Poor boy."

"Luc?" mouthed Piaf. The liar was speaking the truth: today, and every other day since his misfortune, Luc needed Maman's care. And Maman always *needed* to care – too much so, truth be known. Piaf could even feel it now: given Piaf's small size, Maman would wrap her protective strings around her daughter, tight as a spool of thread, until she could hardly breathe. But the stranger's words, so close-to-home, cast proper doubt across Piaf's thinking. *Did* she know him?

With its shiny shell yet to be slit, the fallen chestnut rattled in the pan as the steam within it built and built and built. And, as it rattled, so too did the tiny wooden boxes Piaf imagined were in her mind. Each one, a *memory box*. She stopped fidgeting and shuffling her bare feet on the box beneath her, there to grant her some height. She didn't reach for her button this time and, like freeing a dog of its rope, set her mind free.

Quick as a wink, Piaf's thoughts raced down her memory's alleyways, its maze of thin tunnels, jumping from memory box to memory box until, somewhere deep in her brain, it found the box labelled 1883: five years earlier. She lifted its imaginary lid and allowed her mind to flick through the days inside. *Flick, flick, flick.*

She found it: All Fools' Day – the day of her seventh birthday.

The day the man said they had met.

"I remember," said Piaf, having twisted her button again. "Hailstones woke me, two presents, fried bread for breakfast, I won the race to the sheets and helped Maman fold them for a spoonful of jam from her good silver spoon." She paused when the staring man seemed to sink down a few inches, like a cat ready to pounce. "I made a mask – papier-mâché – and played football with my brother until his friends came. Hopped escargot on my own until cake for tea – seven candles for him, seven for me. Then bed. No puppets. I do not remember you." Without taking her

8

eyes off him, she too leaned over her roasting cart. She reached for her metal scoop and a cone made of old newspaper. *Business as usual.*

"You are mistaken, little girl," said the man. His upper lip twitched. "Birthdays beyond your last are always a blur. What are you – eleven?"

By default, Piaf stood on her tiptoes and gritted her teeth. "I'm twelve." He squinted then. His Adam's apple rolled the length of his neck, like he'd found her words hard to swallow, or extraordinarily delicious – which, she could not tell. She urgently filled the paper cone with roasted chestnuts.

The burning chestnut hopped high in the pan. Piaf noticed, but left it so.

"Your memory deceives you," the stranger hissed, his mask of sickly sweetness giving way to impatience. "Do as your mother would wish. Come." He reached across the cart and clamped his oily fingers around the shoulder strap of her money bag and pinched her coat tight. A waft of something sickly sweet hit her nose. The strong smell of coffee from Les Deux Magots behind her, singed cloth and glue from Pufont's Button Bijouterie before her, and the burning chestnut between them, each fought for attention but were all beaten back – the smell from the stranger's hand, sweet as one hundred cherry berlingots, drowned them out until she could taste it like soap in her mouth. Piaf turned her head and spat.

The girl with the crooked nose shuffled. Her eyes had opened wide. Piaf squinted. Was the girl's head gently shaking side to side? It was almost not there – like a pulse, quivering the feathers of a brave bird. *Yes.* She was saying *no, don't come.*

Piaf tried to squirm free, but the man tried to nudge her sideways, away from her cart. She attempted to catch the eyes of passers-by as the smell of roasting chestnuts hooked them, but they carried on, seemingly drawn like pilgrims from the rising Tour Eiffel towards the chimes of Notre-Dame cathedral.

The chestnut squealed.

Piaf waited until the man's eye had clamped back onto hers before she spoke. "Starting on All Fools' Day, twelve years ago, I remember everything. EVERYTHING. That was a wet Saturday and that was the day I was born. So no, we have not met before because I do not remember you. Enjoy your chestnuts, Monsieur." Strangely, he looked satisfied and licked his lips. Piaf pressed the cone of chestnuts into his palm and shielded her own eyes with her arm.

The chestnut, fed up waiting for someone to take heed of its warnings, exploded.

A searing pain stabbed Piaf. Her hands felt swollen as they clumsily grabbed at her right ear. Oh, how it ached, it burned. Her sight tunnelled, all sound overwhelmed by a shrill whistle. Still, she watched as the man smacked brazier-hot chestnut flesh from his long neck and raised both hands to his eyes. The girl fell forwards, her hand rising too.

That's when Piaf saw it: a thin chain, tied from his wrist to hers.

The stranger lowered the brim of his hat like he could hide in its shadow, and waited for a gap in the flow of passers-by to join them.

The girl spoke.

"You dropped this," she said, her voice rushed and muffled, and held out her clamped-shut fist. Piaf reached out and something heavy dropped into her palm. Her eyes were dragged down when the girl with the crooked nose raised one foot off the ground and spun like a ballerina, as far as her chain would allow.

Then, the man dragged her away.

Two | Deux

Pufont's Button Bijouterie,
Opposite Piaf's Corner, Paris

"Oh! Ma petite plume! Still as a mouse, now! *Still!*"

"Mice don't sit still, Madame," said Piaf, pain clawing at her ear and rushing her words. She pulled herself up onto Madame Legrand's workbench and tried sitting on her flapping hands but her bitten fingernails snagged the layers of rich cloth beneath her. "And you know I don't sit still, neither. If I did, I'd have to remember, and I don't *want* to remember." She sighed, knowing the man's strangeness was setting off a chain reaction inside her head. She *should* tell Madame of his attempt to steal her, but one glance out the button-shop window towards her still-smoking cart and memory boxes began to clatter: every old, danger-filled memory was being dug up, thanks to that stranger, and they were all fighting for her attention.

To stop them, she twisted her button tight.

As it unspun, memories still threatened. She twisted it again until the skin on her thumb burned. Then she tried counting things: the towers of button boxes that rose either side of her like a cardboard sepia city, and spools of colourful thread stacked neatly by Madame into one giant pyramid. When that didn't work, she looked past the sparkling dust motes and out through the window. She tipped her fingertips twice for each sip of coffee taken by Monsieur Auguste over at Les Deux Magots, three times on each sighting of hats with full feathered birds amongst the bustling crowds, and nodded each time breath steamed from the nostrils of hardworking horses as they heaved their carriages out from a fog-filled pothole where Rue du Dragon met Boulevard Saint-Germain. She counted, she fidgeted, she twisted her button. But underneath it all, an uncontrollable worry trembled deep inside. A hug from Maman would be good right now, and it urged Piaf to lean closer to their dear family friend, wishing she could hide in the folds of Madame's colourful djellaba robe.

"Even stiller, ma petite Piaf," said Madame Legrand as she cupped her huge hand beneath Piaf's chin. "Burning chestnut shell INSIDE YOUR EAR is not a good thing. If you want me to fix you, ma plume, you must try to stop fidgeting."

"I am trying," said Piaf, but when she did, even a tiny bit, memories of the stranger seeped like water from a fountain's cracked stone. Her ear pounded. Her mind pounded. Who *was* he? How did he know about her brother, Luc? Was he *the* Parisian child snatcher – the one people had all but ceased to believe was out there? So many children had vanished – *gifted* children. Dates ricocheted across her mind; every few weeks over the last year, news of another lost child had dominated *Le Petit Parisien* headlines, relegating the usual reports on the stolen Cabinet of Oils and its curious history to mere snippets.

"Your poor Maman will be vexed with me for letting this happen," said Madame Legrand. "You know how she worries since she lost your Papa. I promised to keep an eye on you while she visits your poor brother, but half of Paris and dear Monsieur Pufont have kept me too busy!" As always, Piaf spotted the tiny hint of a smile on Madame's lips as soon as she'd mentioned the shop keeper's name. "Look what arrived overnight!" Madame flicked her hand towards a long rack of fancy garments, from long silk gloves and dresses with too many flounces, to stiff overcoats being readied for the winter months ahead; each item hung perfectly parallel to the next, patiently awaiting the latest Pufont Button Bijouterie buttons.

"Please don't tell Maman," said Piaf. She could already feel Maman's protective strings squeezing her arm and reeling her away from her corner on Rue du Dragon. Her freedom, her independence, was at stake.

Madame wiped her hands in the tail of her colourful headscarf and agreed to say nothing without saying so. She attempted to part Piaf's feathery hair. "Hmm. This is a job for Empress Josephine," she appeared to tell the large wooden cabinet on the far side of her workspace. She glanced about the empty shop as though checking for thieves, and whispered, "I hid her in there for safe-keeping."

Piaf stretched herself, as tall as a sitting cat, to see inside the cabinet – she was sure Madame could have happily lived inside it with all its keepsakes and tools, bags of spice and shiny terracotta cooking pots, and not in her grand château that she'd mentioned, with a vague flick of her hand, was out there somewhere. Madame rummaged, Piaf bit her fingernail. Who, or what, was Empress Josephine?

"Here she is," said Madame. A rusty old pair of shears was produced, big enough to cut curtains. "I named her this morning – a fitting title, don't you agree?"

"You are not putting that near my ear!"

"Stop your fretting, ma petite plume!" said Madame Legrand, "All morning I've been snipping yarn with this brute, even Monsieur Pufont's Japanese thread, finer than spider silk!" She waved her shears towards a tailor's dummy fitted with a velvet corset partially adorned with the tiniest buttons.

Piaf squinted – each button was embroidered with a red, blue and white cockade emblem much like a flower. Papa used to wear one on his cap. Memory boxes neatly stacked with everything Papa had told her about the great revolution that had stormed the streets of Paris almost one hundred years prior swayed proudly. Piaf reached out and poked the top button. "They must be wearing this for the Exposition Universelle celebrations next year. It will be one hundred years since our people stormed the Bastille."

"Not yet," said Madame, "that's the year after." Before Piaf could argue dates, Madame had placed the shears flat on her palms for Piaf to see all of them and tapped their underside with her silver rings – *tap, tap, tap* – a trick Maman had taught Madame years ago should she ever need to keep Piaf's attention. Madame tilted the shears back and forth so the low sunlight could do its trick and make their one remaining gem sparkle. Mud had gathered in circles where more gemstones once lay and scratches criss-crossed the blades as though generations of cats had used them to sharpen their claws. It smelt of old metal and spice.

"You should be honoured to have the Empress anywhere near your ear. She's special." Madame Legrand's headscarf threatened to unwind as she peered down upon it. "Empress Josephine probably plucked thorns from the Lord's crown itself," she announced, closing her eyes and raising the shears up. She looked all holy.

Piaf flinched. It was a rule in their household not

to talk of faith, nor glorify it, for doing so gave the wrong people too much power according to Papa. She decided to say nothing. Besides, she didn't know much about religion and the age of things. But she knew an antique when she saw one. "They're old!" she finally said.

Madame purred. "I found them last night – in the grounds of Notre-Dame cathedral," she said, raising her head on the mention of such a place. "There is a reason for everything, ma petite plume… there is even a reason for a mishap." Madame pinched her headscarf and used two fingers to part her hairline to reveal a shining bump.

"Oh!"

"I fell. I *could* blame the bulging roots of *Robinia pseudoacacia*. Have you met her? She's Paris's oldest tree, and her roots run all the way from Square René-Viviani to Notre-Dame." Piaf loved how Madame's voice swirled like birdsong, "But when I rose from the ground, the Lord himself, or your Papa from above, had pressed *these* into my hands. The *real* reason for my fall." Piaf reached for its blade. "NON! You will slice off your finger! See how their point hooks around? *Thread trimming*. Which reminds me," she said, as she cocked her head to one side and whisked her fingers through Piaf's hair. "You could do with a trim while we're at it." She looked up at the cuckoo clock over the door. "We have a few minutes before Monsieur Pufont joins us. Something different, oui? One less job for your Maman, poor soul, busy visiting Luc in Hôtel-Dieu every day… but I'm sure they'll let your brother home any day now."

Any day now? How could Madame scatter hope so flippantly, like fistfuls of cheap birdfeed the old ladies in the Jardin des Tuileries threw? Piaf's twin brother was *not* about to suddenly recover. It had been a long year and nine days since that day; the day he disappeared. Not physically, of course – Luc was still here. It might have sounded impossible, but it was true: Luc had entirely disappeared from *himself.*

Yes, he could walk about, scratch an itch and rub his chin in that annoying way he always did. Every fact from every book and every poem he'd ever written was still there, stuck in his book-worm head, but, when it came to real-life stories, there was nothing; inside, he had no memories, no history of his own. Just like that one time when Piaf opened a spiky chestnut, picked

19

fresh from the tree, to find nothing inside – without his memories, Luc was an empty shell.

Piaf picked up a stick of Madame's tailor's chalk and snapped it in two, for they had been snapped apart too. "Hôtel-Dieu. Stupidest name for an asylum," she managed.

"*Asylum?* Non, Piaf, hush! Don't say that! Your brother is in Hôtel-Dieu, the *hospital*. The asylum is *beneath* it, in old dungeons they say – little more than a jail for the unfortunate few that cannot be..." She blessed herself with her shears.

"Madame?" said Piaf. Madame knew well that Luc's doctor had insisted he be moved to 'dungeon' number three for 'long-term studies' as he'd called them – hadn't Madame visited Luc there many a time over the last year? Piaf's memory boxes rattled, ready to provide dates to prove it, but the sound of Empress Josephine's blades being readied stole her attention.

Using her flat palm, Madame Legrand tilted Piaf's head and snipped.

Piaf jerked.

"Ah, less of that! I only cut hair, see!" She snipped again and waved several inches of wispy brown hair before Piaf's eyes. "At least now I can *see* your ear." She secured the shears in her armpit while she stretched Piaf's ear and peered inside. "Yes, I see it. What were you thinking, letting a chestnut explode?" Madame tutted like she was calling in hens for slops, then sighed. "I know it must be hard managing the roaster on your own. *And* you've not been at it very long. Don't worry, Luc will be back, and all will be saved." The hooked tip of the shears was in Piaf's ear and, without drama, Madame expertly removed the spike of burnt shell.

Piaf rubbed her ear and huffed; its pain suddenly replaced by the sting of Madame's words. *Not at it very long? All will be saved?* Madame made it sound like Luc was the only chestnut roaster in the whole of Paris. So customers didn't chit-chat with her the way they did with Luc. She felt heat rise in her cheeks. No one else knew the precise angle to split a chestnut's glossy skin, or what the perfect weight for freshness was. Or how chestnuts housed with a twin were always the best – they had to fight harder to grow so always had a bit of a bite about them.

"I've been 'at it' on my own for over a year," she finally spat, "and I *let* that chestnut explode! Luc would've too – that man was trying to steal me!"

Newspapers flapped like flags over memory boxes in her mind, each headline reporting the disappearance of another child. *Twenty*, Piaf counted. Twenty times over the last year, reporters stopped incessantly dwelling on the mystery of the missing Cabinet of Oils to report that a child had been stolen. A *gifted* child. Monsieur Pufont's grandson and apprentice, Bertrand, to name one. Piaf always wondered if the same headline space would be afforded to a gift-less child, such as her. Only for the exploding chestnut, tomorrow's newspaper might have answered that.

Madame Legrand turned Piaf's head so that they were face-to-face.

"What man?" The whites of Madame's eyes and their spidery veins never looked so large. Piaf could not answer. While Monsieur Pufont's footsteps thudded across the floor above, the only question that thudded up and down the narrow tunnels in Piaf's mind, knocking on every memory box in search of an answer, was *Why?*

Why would a snatcher of *gifted* children want someone like her?

Three | Trois

"Answer me, Piaf, ma plume!" Madame Legrand tugged at Piaf's cuff, urging her to twist her button, and focus. "WHAT man?"

Piaf gasped as her attention returned to Madame. She spoke fast: "The stranger. He was telling me to go with him... that he knew me, said he was Maman's cousin. He had a girl with a crooked nose chained to him, Madame! And he even tried to pull me by my strap!" A memory box quickly reminded her how his fingers smelled of cherry berlingots, so she placed her thumb beneath the strap's leather and raised it to her own nose. "It still stinks! Smell it, Madame! He said we met on my birthday, when I was seven. Please don't tell Maman."

"You met?"

"No. He was lying. I checked my seventh birthday, Madame, and he wasn't there. So, I let the chestnut explode."

"Perhaps another birthday then?" suggested Madame Legrand. She stared at Piaf's forehead, waiting for her memory to do its trick.

Piaf tapped a finger against her own temple. "Every box in there was as still as your mice. No rattling."

Madame Legrand wrapped an arm around Piaf's head. She hugged Piaf tight, losing her for a moment in her robe's folds, but she said no more. At first Piaf thought that was proof that there was nothing to worry about – it was simply a strange meeting with a strange man – but, as Madame continued snipping at her hair, Piaf stole glances at the thin silver medals that hung in rows from Madame's silk headscarf; instead of dancing side-to-side against her smooth skin, they were balanced awkwardly against the deepest furrows that now lined her forehead.

"Madame?"

Madame Legrand wiped the blades of Empress Josephine on her spice-speckled robe and turned to face the window. She glanced across the narrow, cobbled road towards Piaf's corner where the roasting cart stood unmanned. "Perhaps you will move your roaster a little closer to the shop tomorrow, ma petit plume. Your Maman was right to fret – Parisian corners might not be safe for an eleven-year-old."

Eleven-year-old? Feeling smaller than before, Piaf tutted. Yes, she was small. So small, in fact, she'd been wrapped in a handkerchief and placed in an open drawer as soon as she was born. "Un *piaf*," the midwife had whispered. "A *sparrow*, ready to fledge its nest and leave us." Small as she was, she did survive, only to always be assumed fragile and younger than her years. But Madame should know better than that.

"You've forgotten I'm twelve." Taking a leaf out of her brother's book, Piaf hadn't bothered to soften her words – it was, after all, a matter of fact – but her tone was too sharp, and she suddenly felt like a bird imitating the song of another. Perhaps Madame was in shock; the distance between Piaf's roaster and the button shop was short and the chestnut explosion *was* loud – loud as a gunshot. That would explain Madame's forgetfulness. Madame would apologise, any moment now. Rather than look Madame in the eye, Piaf pressed her finger against the sample buttons stitched to the front of every cardboard box within

25

reach. They reminded her of cherry-knocking on her favourite Parisian doorbells.

"Don't be in such a hurry to grow up, Piaf," said Madame, "Eleven is a good age, but twelve is an important one. I already have a special surprise planned for your twelfth birthday."

Piaf recoiled. Madame had *properly* forgotten her age. And, a memory box in her mind was quick to flag that Madame had also forgotten the Exposition Universelle celebrations were next year, not the year after like she had said. It drove Piaf to distraction how people could simply forget things when she had no choice but to remember it all, reliving the bad and the ugly time and again. How did they even do that – *forgetting*? And surely her twelfth birthday wasn't that forgetful. With her fingers and frustration, Piaf reached across Madame's workbench and nudged one of the perfectly lined up Russian dolls filled with thimbles. She spun it around and around, just as the girl with the crooked nose had done before the man dragged her away. "*Twelve*."

Madame nudged the Russian doll back into its proper place. "Are you *really* telling me you are twelve years old?"

"Yes," said Piaf. She squinted at Madame. The furrows were back, and this time they rolled like the ripples on the River Seine. She must have been having what Maman would call a *bad day*. Or perhaps all this talk of strangers and child snatchers brought back unwanted memories of Monsieur Pufont's grief when his grandson, Bertrand, went missing. Piaf knew Madame cared deeply for the button shop owner. She also knew how it felt to have bad memories haunting, again and again. "Sorry, Madame." Piaf stared at Madame, curious about her thoughts. "You think that stranger stole Bertrand, don't you?"

"Pardon?"

"*Bertrand*, Madame. Maybe I met his snatcher."

"Monsieur Pufont's Bertrand? Bertie Pufont?" Madame's voice was higher pitched than usual, like someone was standing on her toe. "Bertie is upstairs, ma plume. Monsieur Pufont is probably trying to get his lazy bones out of bed, right this minute." Madame waved her hand at the cuckoo clock, "It is about time."

Piaf froze. Madame was not well! Bertrand Pufont went missing ten months ago. Forgetting her twelfth birthday was a big thing, but forgetting Bertrand's disappearance? The shop had even closed for two weeks before Christmas, so distraught was his grandfather. He'd stopped eating entirely until Madame brought him strange, spiced dishes cooked in her château's great kitchen. Not sure what to say, Piaf twisted and twisted her squirrel button, carved by Bertrand's gifted hand. Piaf had never met the boy – he had hidden himself in Pufont's shop, carving buttons instead of dealing with the real world that had only weeks prior stolen his poor parents. But, as Piaf studied the care and attention he'd placed into every fine line of her squirrel button, she'd felt like she knew him. Then, he'd disappeared.

Suddenly, Madame's palm was across Piaf's forehead. "Piaf. How long have you been roasting chestnuts without Luc?" There was a pause. "Just answer."

"A year and nine days. Madame, it is not *me* who is unwell."

"A year? I thought you said that earlier." Madame whistled like a kettle on the boil. "What year is it, Piaf?"

"Madame? There is nothing wrong with me." Piaf shook her head – Madame was being a worry-worm, same as Maman. Piaf stilled as Maman's voice echoed in her mind, saying her petite daughter wouldn't be able to climb the Tour Eiffel that was being built for the Exposition Universelle this spring. "You'll slip through the gaps like a floating feather," she had said. "And besides, think of the crowds, ma petite fille," she'd added, before crushing a poppy seed between her fingers.

Madame slapped Piaf's hand, grabbing back her wandering attention. "The year?"

Piaf snorted – Madame would ask what her name was next. "I'm *fine!* And it's 1888." Perhaps Madame had forgotten that too?

"Non. Non. Non. It's *1887.*"

Piaf gulped. Poor Madame looked pained – perhaps forgetting things hurt sometimes. Piaf needed proof – that would help Madame remember. She ran for the door.

"Piaf! Get back here! You are ill!"

"I am NOT ill, Madame Legrand!" cried Piaf as she ran in the same direction as the flow of passers-by. "It's 1888, not 1887." She ran across the narrow road, past her roasting cart on her corner at Rue du Dragon, and beyond to the crowded nest of coffee tables outside Les Deux Magots. Each had its own newspaper, neatly folded by Monsieur Auguste and tucked between a silver jug and bowl of sugar cubes. Apologising to a diner, she grabbed a newspaper and whipped it open. "Oh. *1887.*" Then another and another until Monsieur Auguste flapped his hands and Madame whistled for her return.

Piaf slapped her forehead with the butt of her palm. "Of course! It's a mistake! And they'd all have the wrong date, wouldn't they?" She snorted. How silly – papers were always printed together, weren't they? Any mistake in one would appear in the other. She chewed her lip. "But I can still prove it's 1888…" she yelled, hoping her voice would dodge the crowded footpath and reach Madame's forgetful ears. She dashed back towards her roasting cart.

She flicked a shard of exploded shell from the pyramid of chestnuts' flank and then grabbed all the evidence she needed: her tower of newspaper cones.

"I collected these from Pierre's stall this morning – *yesterday's* newspapers!" As she stepped away from her cart, she rolled out the top cone and, having found the printed date, held it up, smiling.

"Yes, Madame! 1888!" she confirmed and did a quick dance. It was not her who was losing her mind!

She searched out Madame through the crowd. When she saw her, Madame's hands were pressed against her cheeks. Piaf could see Monsieur Pufont by her side. He looked worried.

He waved his top hat at her. "Have you seen my Bertie this morning?" he cried.

Before Piaf took a step towards Pufont's Button Bijouterie, a rattling sound grabbed her attention from behind. As she watched her roaster's precious pyramid of chestnuts collapse into the pan – slowly at first, and then faster and faster – she felt the ground beneath her feet shake.

She looked down at the cobbles.

The swirling morning fog had scarpered, tickling her bare toes as it was sucked down through the gaps between stones. One cobble sank downwards too, an inch or so, sending a tiny puff of dirt skywards, then another and another. Like standing on a hot pan, she hopped from foot to foot before the floor of cobbles entirely disappeared before her eyes. She cast one last glance across the narrow road towards Madame Legrand and Monsieur Pufont, as the ground opened up and swallowed her whole.

Four | Quatre

Beneath Piaf's Corner, Rue du Dragon, Paris

D own, Piaf fell.
Down.

Down, and down, past rock and bone. Dust and sharp edges, grit between her teeth, and a thudding and rumbling, deep as thunder. Then darkness. Darkness, until a row of thin silver medals dangling from a headscarf of silk caressed her cheek and bolted her awake.

Like a cat at a bird, Piaf scrambled for Madame's headscarf. But it flew away as the earth shook again and rocks and dirt rained down from above. Piaf clamped her arms around her head and pulled her knees up to her chest until she was tiny as a bug, and she rolled. She rolled and rolled, over rubble and fallen chestnuts, clanging her feet off her roaster's crumpled metal brazier, and scuffing her knees and her elbows until she found shelter, somewhere. The earth rumbled one last time and, when a wall of rock thumped down and cracked and smashed before her, all light disappeared.

Was she in hell?

She reached out, and clawed and clawed at the wall of rock and earth. "Help!" she tried to cry, but dust smothered her voice and matted her lashes shut. "I'm down here," she croaked, over and over. Goodness knows how long she dug and hammered until she finally stopped and held her breath. There was not a sound. No one was coming. "Don't forget me."

She grappled at the strap of her money bag, now pulled taut about her neck. She heaved it downwards and the cherry berlingot stench from the stranger's fingers coated the dust in the air until it crunched between her teeth. Every godforsaken dangerous memory banged and rattled in her mind, but she knew this memory in the making would haunt her for ever.

She dug her hand deep into her bag and pulled out her silver box of brazier matches. She lit one; it snuffed out. She lit another, carefully scooting it about. There at her bare feet was a tooth-coloured bone, one the length of her forearm. Dust extinguished the match's flame again, so she pulled and dragged at her torn sleeve, ripping its cuff until she held a stretch of material in her hand. She wrapped it around the bone's top and held it like a torch. The shredded threads from her lost squirrel button were the first to catch the flame of the next match.

She could see.

Her heart pummelled in her chest, every muscle shook. She was buried, underground.

She was crouching low beneath arched rock.

"Help!" she cried at the wall of buttery-yellow rock before her, and, this time, her voice was loud. She leapt when her call echoed on and on. She turned, holding the torch of burning cuff and bone out before her.

A stone tunnel, like the ones she imagined were in her mind, stretched out ahead. The darkness stole its length and she shrieked when, in that darkness, she saw a storm of golden lights, tiny as fireflies. Second by second, more appeared, and larger and larger they became. *Eyes*.

Something knocked the torch from her hand and all light was suddenly snuffed out. Blackness, as black as black can be, until the ground heaved and retched, over and over, and only stopping when a dagger of light finally broke through. With it, came something: Madame's scarf floated down once again, its row of silver medals flashing like falling stars. This time, Piaf would catch it.

Five | Cinq

Room Three, Basement Floor, Hôtel-Dieu, Paris

There was a grubby handwritten list of twenty things, each sentence numbered.

"Number One: Your name is Luc Durand," the boy read with one eye open. His voice was hoarse, coming and going in waves. He leaned up on his elbow and rubbed sleep from his eyes. *"Two: You are from Evron, but now live in Paris. Three: Your mother will visit every day – you call her 'Mother', sometimes 'Maman'."* There was a noise, a ring tapping off metal, perhaps. He looked over to the corner of the small room where

a grey-haired, tired-looking woman sat pin-straight in a hard chair.

He reached over to where the list was posted on the side of his bedside table and used his fingernail to lever out its brass drawing pin. It tinkled to the ground. He peered over the side of his bed, and, amongst cotton balls and fluff and a dusty brown leather suitcase, he saw several more pins. Some were trodden on and spike-less, dotted across the terracotta tiled floor.

"Déjà vu. I've done this before," he realised, and a dread filled his stomach when the woman slowly nodded. Sitting up, he used his damp hands to flatten out the note's wrinkles and laid it on the bedsheets before him.

He read on, out loud: "*Your twin sister visits too. And it says the word *Piaf*. Is that her name?"

The woman nodded. "Our little sparrow," she said, and smiled.

He continued reading, "*She is shorter than you. You are both twelve*. That's point number four," he said to the woman, wanting her to confirm or deny. Could this all be true?

The woman looked confused. She picked up her

tapestry bag and rummaged through it. Armed with a pencil, she approached the bed and looked at the list. She scribbled out "twelve", replacing it with "eleven". "Pardon, Luc. I… I must have made a mistake. You are eleven." She nodded at Luc to continue reading and returned to her chair.

The boy's eye jumped down past several other points to the last line, unnumbered and written in uppercase letters: *THE DOCTORS ARE HERE TO HELP YOU. DO NOT BE AFRAID.*

And so, he was.

"Pardon," he said to the woman and gulped. Suddenly, he felt strangled, uncomfortable. He fought the urge to open his pyjama shirt's top button. "I am lost." There was no other way to describe it.

"For several days, my love. Since the sixteenth day of October." The woman's voice was new to him, yet so loving. It felt odd.

He ran his hands through his curly hair and read the note again, this time in his head.

"I am Luc?" he asked the woman, but raised his hand before she had a chance to reply. He didn't know the woman at all, and he'd want to argue this fact, tooth and nail, should the woman say it were

38

true. If he *were* Luc – he'd know it, wouldn't he? He scratched around in his mind looking for proof: *What is my name? Who am I?* The only answers he had were written on the paper before him. "I… am Luc," he finally repeated, hoping it would somehow ring true.

The woman nodded. "You are my Luc."

"And you are my…" He checked his list again, "my… Maman?" He felt heat rise in his cheeks – perhaps some part of him was embarrassed. Much to his surprise, he began to cry. "Where am I?"

"Hôtel-Dieu – when I arrived this morning, I could not find you at first," the woman said, a flash of remembered panic scrunching her eyes, "The doctors had moved you… to the *basement*, overnight." Her head dipped and it did not go unnoticed.

It did not matter to Luc which building or floor he was on. "But, where am *I*?" He hammered his fist against his temple. "I can't think! I am totally lost."

"It is your memories that are lost, not you, and it happened out of the blue." The woman, his mother, raised her hands and eyes up to the grey ceiling. "You were doing the chestnut gathering that morning because Piaf's boot needed mending." His mother must have noticed his confusion because she slid over to the bedside and gently pointed towards the list. "It's point number six – you are a chestnut roaster, Luc, and you should be proud – you are the best roaster in the city. Your Papa taught you how, and your sister helps you. But one day, you didn't come home. Piaf found you, next to a fallen tree."

"Did I bang my head? Is that what happened?"

"We do not know – there was no evidence of any head injury. But you are not *unwell* – you have your health, fit as a horse, so they say. And you have a family who loves you. You also have the best doctor in the world – he heard of your plight, this memory specialist. You are fortunate, my son. Dr Le Chandelier is one of the great minds brought to Paris to unlock the mysteries of Rapiditus's Cabinet of Oils. A healer, a scientist and a philosopher are on the team, but everyone knows Dr Le Chandelier is the real mastermind," she said, seemingly proud. "And *he* calls you his 'wondrous enigma' – that means you too are a mystery—"

"I understand the word." This fact surprised him. How could he remember that and not simple things, like who he was?

"Of course you do; you were always a very bright

boy. You rarely have your head out of a book and that's all still in there." She pointed to his head and then tilted her own to one side. Staring at Luc, the woman smiled as though pleased with a work of art. "Dr Le Chandelier says that all of you is still intact, Luc – your intelligence, your awareness and judgement. He has tested you and says you are a smart boy." She seemed to raise her chin with pride but to Luc there was little to be proud of. A smart boy who didn't know his own name? "The doctor says your memory is still in there, somewhere, but it is hiding. It is locked away. They are doing many tests to fix you, my son, some less than easy for you." She paused to search her sleeve for a handkerchief and blew her nose. When she spoke again, her voice was higher – upset, he realised. "Until they figure out their little enigma, I'm afraid each time you wake up, all will be entirely new to you."

"Each time I wake up?" Luc attempted a pretend smile. "Like a fresh start?" He'd said it because the woman needed cheering up; in fact, he wanted to say more, much more, but he did not have time – someone panting to his right stole his attention.

A short, barefoot child, all flitty and disorganised as a pile of dried leaves on a windy day, appeared in

41

the doorway, bracing themselves either side with their hands. Was it a boy? No – a girl, Luc decided. Like a fledgling yet to grow into its feathers, her coat was too large, its waistband hanging low by her hips. She wore baggy trousers probably fashioned from a dress. They were strangely tied tight at their ends and shoved up high above her knees where scabs, some fresh, some old and picked at, poked out from her dusty skin.

Seconds later, a curtain of shiny colours swayed in behind her – no, not a curtain… it was a woman – a giant woman, as wide and tall as the door. She planted her hands and kisses on the girl's head, wailing something about miracles and how she thought the girl was dead. When she let go, she stood there, heaving long, wheezy breaths, fanning the barefoot girl's wild hair with each exhale.

Like a magnet, his eyes were drawn back to the girl. She was *filthy*. Her feet shuffled, her head shook. Each finger tapped wildly out of sync with each other at the peeling varnish of the door frame. Then he saw her eyes – two of the brightest, nicest eyes he might have ever seen.

Luc sat bolt upright. "PIAF?"

Six | Six

Piaf broke free of Madame Legrand's grasp and ran awkwardly, like the first flight of a bird, to Maman.

"What happened? PIAF?"

Piaf coughed, stuck words etched in her dusty throat. Maman leaned forward in her chair and, with fear and open palms, scanned Piaf's ruffled, flapping body. Piaf looked down upon herself: ripped clothing stood out at odd angles, and she was covered in a yellow dust that darkened to a rust where it seeped into sweat and clumped into stinging cuts on her legs and the back of her hands.

Maman would never let her out of her sight again. Despite Piaf's every inclination, she had to play this down.

"I fell," said Piaf. It wasn't a lie, and she hoped it would do. A throb hammered at her ear, her ankle too. Something buzzed through her veins. It was so terribly frightening and deliciously exciting all at once. "A *big* fall."

Maman's speedy prayers and trembling hands told Piaf her explanation wouldn't do.

More words bubbled on Piaf's tongue, but she bit down on them; just like her rattling and stomping memories, she too wanted to scream how the ground had opened up like a big mouth and swallowed her, threatening her with a swarm of golden eyes before spitting her out. But, more importantly, she wanted to scream about what happened before that: the stranger – how he brazenly tried to tug her away and how another victim was chained to him. A victim she'd made no effort to help! But telling Maman all this would take Piaf away from her corner on Rue du Dragon, whatever was left of it, and it would chain *her* to this room for ever. She would sit here, like Maman, staring at Luc, feeling her heart break a little bit more every time he woke up and forgot who he was. How did Maman face it, day in, day out, for over a year?

"You'll be the death of me," Maman said, like always, but the hug Piaf so desperately needed, came. Like being tucked into bed, she felt rooted, and hung on tight. Too tight, perhaps, and too still. She managed a quick wave at Luc before memories took advantage and overwhelmed her. Bones, and falling down; down potholes on a bicycle when she was nine, down Papa's ladder, down branch after branch in the Jardin des Tuileries, down the stairs in Galeries Lafayette, down from a chair as a curious toddler – memories bounced around her head, searching for somewhere to settle. And, each time, she imagined the stranger, with his dangling gold button and a chain about his wrist, shoving her. Her body jerked several times as she relived each fall over and over.

She felt the tickle of her mother's voice, whispering in her ear. "Piaf. *Piaf?*" she called, as Piaf's face twisted and reddened at everything her memory was replaying.

Piaf gasped as her attention returned to the room. Maman squeezed her as tight as a hen for the pot. Tight enough to stop any stranger from tugging her away – not even an inch.

"Maybe try twisting your squirrel button?" said Maman, "And what did you do to your hair?" Maman pulled a wispy lock from each side out wide, one several inches longer than the other.

"Blame Empress Josephine," said Piaf.

Bent forward and leaning against the door frame to catch her breath, Madame Legrand tutted and pulled the tip of her new shears from a pocket hidden somewhere in her swaying robe. "My scissors. She escaped from my clutches before I—"

"And I lost my button! Down there!" said Piaf, pointing to the floor. "In hell!" She dangled her ripped cuff towards her mother's face – a face still muddled and flattened with worry. Piaf sighed and wiped dust and a little bit of regret from her own face – so maybe it wasn't quite the mouth of hell, but there *were* bones. It *was* scary.

Maman's eyebrows met like a bow readied for its arrow. There was more to what had happened than a *big fall*, and she knew it. She fired a loaded glance at Madame Legrand.

"Rosetta," said Maman to Madame Legrand. "Tell me what happened?" Piaf pulled Maman's face back to meet hers, but it sprung back to face Madame.

Madame reached for a tumbler of water on a tray inside the door and gulped it down. "Oh, mon amie!"

she began, but paused when she heard the rustle of paper as Luc reached for his list of twenty things. "Un moment," she said to Maman. "Luc. You have a new room – all to yourself." She stomped, breathlessly, towards him.

"TOO HEAVY, MADAME!" warned Piaf, feeling the thud of Madame's feet through the asylum's old terracotta tiles. Knowing what stood only inches below them, she lifted her own feather-light feet, dancing like they were on a bed of eggshells. "We have to walk *lightly*. The ground is so thin, like a shell."

"Luc," said Madame Legrand. Like wiping tears from a toddler, she gently rubbed her palm along the length of Luc's confused face, "I am Madame Rosetta Legrand. We are friends." She pointed towards number eight on his list before pointing to Piaf and Maman. "I need to talk to your mother and your whirling dervish of a sister." She spun her finger around like a spinning top, and Luc's head of tight curls danced with it. "This is not how she normally looks. Not quite, anyway." She turned her attention to Maman. "Disaster, mon amie, in Paris! We're lucky to still have her." Madame blessed herself and sank the end of Luc's bed to half its height as she sat.

She was ready to tell Maman *everything*.

Piaf sighed. Maman's arms, still wrapped about her, suddenly felt like a cage. And, with every word that would fall from Madame's mouth, Piaf would feel her freedom fly far, far away.

Seven | Sept

"Your daughter was swallowed up by a hole, almost as big as my kitchen," said Madame Legrand. "Only for my long scarf…" She pulled down the hood of her djellaba and pointed at her head. It was now scarf-less, though her matted black curls still held the shape of it. "There was a sound like a giant heaving a great sigh, then a hole opened up and Rue du Dragon disappeared – but, mon amie," she said and reached for Maman's hand. "Before all that happened…"

Madame Legrand pointed at the tumbler of water by the door, instructing Piaf to bring it to her. It was empty of course, but Piaf knew Madame wanted Maman alone. Piaf twitched herself free of Maman and hovered for a bit, watching Madame lean even closer to her mother, before leaving them be. Madame lowered her voice to a failed whisper. "I think she is not well, Marie! Her *memory*. She thinks it is already 1888!"

"*My* memory?" Piaf hissed under her breath, quiet enough for Madame's ears not to hear, but loud enough for Luc's eyes to widen. Piaf wanted to shout about how it was Madame who was not well; insisting Bertrand Pufont was still around, insisting the long-planned Exposition Universelle was not happening next year but the year after, and for insisting that it was 1887 – it was like she'd forgotten a whole year. But, at least, Madame was not telling of the stranger – Piaf might have freed herself from his clutches, but if Maman knew *that* had happened? Piaf tutted, in the same way Madame would often do, and placed the empty tumbler in Madame's spice-stained palm, upside down to make a point.

On seeing she had the attention of more ears than she'd intended, Madame Legrand whistled like a chatty robin, stood up and reached for Maman. "Oh! Mon amie, your black hair has greyed like a wolf overnight!" she said.

Piaf looked at Maman's hair. There was nothing different about it.

Madame wrapped a strand of Maman's hair around her finger. "A good soaking in my walnut-hull powder will have you looking yourself—"

"*Fontis!*" interrupted Luc, his voice cracking from lack of use. "You're all talking about a *fonti* – a sinkhole, I think." He rubbed his chin. "I read an interesting article once that said it happened before – in 1774 at Rue d'Enfer."

"Rue d'Enfer? The *Street of Hell?*" gasped Piaf. Maybe she really had been to hell. She chewed her swollen lip, picked at her nails. And maybe hell didn't want her there. Or didn't even *notice* her there. That's why it spat her back out. A box, heaviest of all and weighed down with sad thoughts, unhinged its lid. The memories inside it told her there was nothing new about how hell had treated her; she was well used to being either ignored or unnoticed, given her small height, or frankly unwanted, because of her failure to just sit still.

"The sinkhole was 'the work of the devil, a saint, or a magician'," continued Luc. Piaf could see his eyes trail from left to right as he read from some book stored deep in his mind, "That's what they'd said. They found something strange down there... the—"

51

"Cabinet of Oils…" said Maman, sitting taller.

"…of Saint Rapiditus," said Madame Legrand. She blessed herself.

"*Magician*, not saint," corrected Maman, her face suddenly serious as thunder. Piaf felt pride wash over her – like Papa, Maman didn't take too kindly to the Church claiming anything of such value or intrigue.

Luc had their full attention. "Some say Rapiditus was a saint, some say magician, but either way they were wrong, of course, about what caused the sinkhole. It was the work of Mother Nature. They're holes in the ground – like a cave when its roof collapses. Water can make them – it dissolves the rock beneath the soil and creates an underground cave. And, um," he pointed at Maman's grey hair, "Madame Legrand's walnut hull is a good treatment for stomach worms, too." He patted his head, wondering if everything he had just said really came from it. "What am I? An encyclopaedia?" He grimaced, and then nodded at his sister. "You are Piaf?" The smile that suddenly beamed across his face tickled Piaf's too.

Maman patted Piaf's shoulder and squinted as a cloud of her dust rose. "Go talk to your brother, but take it easy – he has only woken, so he knows little."

52

Maman smiled but her eyebrows hung low as she tried to comprehend Madame Legrand's concern about Piaf's memory.

Piaf limped over to Luc and threw herself onto his bed. Despite her dust, she sat cross-legged on the pillow as though it were her own, and flapped her knees up and down, scrunched her toes – the usual. She saw Luc's eyes jump from her legs to her fingers as they scratched and tapped. She picked at her swollen lip – he didn't mean it, but she still felt a little bit judged.

"I promise you'll get used to it – my fidgeting. Or *fluttering* as you always call it. I can't sit still. Or stand still. If I do, I get lost – in here," she said, pointing to her head. She began to whistle a hectic tune she'd heard when clowns ran amok at the Cirque D'Hiver. Like a bird on a May morning, Luc whistled it too. He reached for his lips. "How do I even know this?"

"The doctor in here said music is safe in the part of your brain that stores all those poems you've written, too – and anything you've learned off by heart. Like facts. Try your times-tables," said Piaf, hurriedly – she was itching to get on with it and tell him the good stuff, like nearly being snatched, for a start. Luc would want to know every detail. "And I've told you all this before – every day since you came here… that's over a year now—"

Madame Legrand grabbed Maman's cheeks with both hands. "Oh, mon amie! Did you hear what she said? *See?*"

"Piaf. No tricks on your brother. You will confuse him. Luc, mon fils, this is your…" Maman totted something up on her fingers, "… *ninth* day."

Piaf gasped.

"Maman! Madame!" Six unblinking eyes stared back at her. "What is WRONG with you today? Luc is here exactly one year and nine days. And, before you say it, Madame, it's 1888." Piaf hid her mouth with her hand and whispered to Luc, "Don't listen to them. You can believe *me* because, since the day we were born, I can remember everything that's happened. It's all in here." She pointed to her head.

Luc stared at her forehead.

Piaf rolled her eyes to express the burden she carried. "*Everything.*"

"Like a list of facts? Like you've written it all down?" Piaf caught his glance at his short list of twenty things.

"Sort of, but with wooden boxes, millions of

them." She poked at her scalp with all ten fingers. "But not *wood* wood. They rattle when a memory wants to be heard – anything can set them off. There are tunnels and shortcuts and alleyways everywhere, and the boxes are linked in so many ways, I get lost sometimes— never mind," she added, cutting herself short when Luc's eyes opened wide.

He rubbed his chin for a moment. "What happened on the seventeenth day of January in, um, 1883?"

"You stubbed your toe on Papa's hammer. He was telling us about an earthquake in Italy at the time, not that you can remember any of this—"

"The sixteenth day of June, then, 1885?" He was staring at Piaf's forehead again.

"Eggs for breakfast. You got a shell."

"Did I? Brilliant! You remember everything!" He rocked side-to-side in excitement, then held his hands either side of Piaf's head like it was a crystal vase on a wobbling shelf. "You're a library – like the Bibliothèque Nationale! With all its shelves and catalogues and archive boxes all squished into your head!"

He'd said it like it was something amazing, something to be proud of.

A power. A *superpower*, even.

Not a burden.

"You're gifted," said Luc, proudly. It was meant kindly, but it slapped awake an unboxed memory in Piaf's mind – the memory that had snaked about from box to box in search of an answer: why would a snatcher of *gifted* children want someone like her?

Piaf shuddered. "Non, Luc. I'm just a girl who can't forget, even if I wanted to."

Eight | Huit

There was a silence between Piaf and Luc, a silence Madame's fraught whispers to Maman could not even penetrate. Piaf let him own it – she guessed he was figuring out how it must feel to be her, and she spent the moment trying to imagine how it felt to be him. Memory-full and memory-less, they were poles apart, yet together, sitting cross-legged on Luc's bed.

When Luc smiled a kind, sad smile, Piaf spoke.

"Maman is wrong. Madame is wrong. You are here more than nine days."

Luc leaned over the side of his bed and started counting something before reaching down. He held up one of many flattened brass drawing pins, just like the one used to hang his list of twenty things. There were way more than nine. "I know."

He believed her.

And he didn't believe Maman. "But why would she say—"

Piaf shrugged – it *was* odd. Maman's memory was normally good. Likewise, Madame was as sharp as the drawing pin against which Piaf now incessantly clicked her thumbnail.

"It's like Maman and Madame have forgotten a whole year," said Piaf. "Their thinking is all messed up." A box rattled, reminding her of an odd conversation she'd had with her mother that morning. "Maman came into our bedroom today. She picked up a cushion, swearing she'd never seen it before. She crocheted it herself only two months ago, Luc. It has stripes so she'd said you'd like it."

"Bizarre," said Luc.

"And that's not the only bizarre thing going on," whispered Piaf. She nudged closer to Luc and checked over his shoulder for eavesdroppers, only to see Madame Legrand doing the very same thing as she ushered Maman out of the room, whispering, no doubt about her.

"A man came to our roaster today." Fearing the raw memory of it would overwhelm her, she reached for a button on her brother's pyjamas and began twisting it. Luc instinctively leaned closer, to make it easier.

"*Our roaster*," said Luc like he was trying out the words. He flicked his head towards Maman's empty chair, "She said I am the best chestnut roaster in Paris."

Piaf struggled to swallow for a second. "She… Maman said that?" She didn't wait for, nor want, his reply. "This man who came to the roaster – he didn't want chestnuts. He wanted me! He was at least three times taller than me," she exaggerated, "but I fought back."

Luc raised an eyebrow.

"It's *true*. He was trying to force me to go with him, but I'm telling you, Luc, I fought like a tiger," she said, adding plenty more spice to what her memory was replaying. "I pushed him off me when he grabbed my strap." Piaf pulled the bag's strap over her head and held it out to her brother. It was only now that she noticed the four lines of oil from the man's fingers that had seeped into the soft leather. "It's our money bag, for all the chestnuts we sell. You normally do the selling, sometimes a bit of picking, but I do all the rest – roasting, deliveries too. I hate talking to customers."

Piaf glanced at Luc, wondering if he was reading

her mind as twins often do. Being so small was her problem, wasn't it? The way people literally spoke down to her, like she wasn't big enough to grow an opinion. Daily, she felt her confidence beaten smaller still – to the size of a pea – making her muddle up words and sound like a fool. She twisted Luc's button again, desperate to keep more memories at bay. "Anyway, sales were looking good – it was like the smell of roasting chestnuts got stuck in all that fog out there. Did you see it, the fog? Here, take the strap. I dare you to smell it – it stinks something rotten, just like him."

Luc held the strap in his hands like an open book, but didn't smell it.

Perched on the bed, Piaf hung her legs over the side and swung them wildly. "So, I blew him up with a chestnut! BANG! And you should've seen the girl chained to him – she was white as a ghost and had a nose like a witch." More spice. "She gave me something." Piaf rummaged through the dust-filled bag between them, speeding up at the growing sound of a doctor's expensive shoes on corridor tiles. Her mother's voice came, too. "Here it is," said Piaf. She held out the girl's gift – a chestnut burr. Thanks to the sinkhole, it was now a ball of dried, butter-coloured mud and grit, sharp spikes poking out at odd angles.

Luc rubbed his chin. "A chestnut? It's in its spiky burr – its overcoat," he said, unable to restrain the need to express facts – they were, after all, all he had.

Piaf held it up and studied it properly for the first time. "The girl with the crooked nose said I'd dropped it." She weighed it for freshness on her flat palm. It was a large one, heavy, and therefore probably fresh – as though it had just fallen.

Other than that, it was entirely odd.

For a start, it shouldn't have been there. "We never bring chestnut burrs to our cart, Luc! We open them where they're picked, in the Jardin des Tuileries. Maman doesn't like the mess and the spikes get into her slippers. Wait!" Using her fingernail, she dragged it along the chestnut's bristly spikes, sending a shower of crumbling mud bed bound. There was little give in them, and they tinkled quietly, like Maman's bone comb. "This is not a real chestnut. It's been carved out of wood!"

Luc took the wooden burr and turned it over and over in his hands, allowing the remaining dust and grit to fall through his fingers. He held it up between them and pointed to its shell of countless perfectly pointed wooden spikes, each almost thin as a hair.

"And it came from a witch-girl." Piaf jumped down off the bed and spun on one foot, just as the girl had done before she had been dragged away. "A chained-up witch-girl who twirled like a ballerina just before hell opened its mouth." Piaf found herself biting her lip, having perhaps overdone it. "But I think *she* was probably nice."

"Why was the girl chained to the man?"

"Because he stole her. Like he tried to steal me. And I bet he stole Bertrand Pufont, too; he was thirteen and he was the boy who worked in the button shop. We tried to get him to come out and play more than once but he was too sad, I guess," she added, and quickly explained how Madame and, now that she thought about it, his grandfather Monsieur Pufont, seemed to think the boy was never taken.

"A smelly child snatcher and a ballerina witch-girl in chains. Are you making this up? Is this a test of some sort?" Luc glanced around as though seeking out someone keeping score.

Piaf raised the strap of the money bag to her brother's nose. "If you don't believe me, then smell it – it still stinks. That smell came from the man's fingers and that's what a snatcher smells like—" Piaf held her breath – she'd heard her mother whimper, outside in the corridor. She tiptoed to the door and listened for a bit but gave up when the doctor's words to her mother got too complicated and boring. The tip of the great man's shadow soon reached the threshold of the door.

"They're coming," said Piaf. She ran back to her brother, quickly stuffed the burr back into her bag and sat back up on the bed. She left her feet dangling, and sat on her hands, just as Maman would prefer.

The doctor marched in, bringing with him a draught and a nurse.

Piaf gulped – where was Maman? Without her, she wouldn't know how to speak to a proper doctor! Especially one like Dr Le Chandelier! He was a genius who Maman strangely called "a household name". Piaf had never heard a house named like that, but it was no wonder she was always ushered out when he did his rounds – he was the man chosen to lead the team of experts studying Rapiditus's Cabinet of Oils. Whether a saint or a magician, Rapiditus was a man known for his swift "miracles" going back hundreds of years, and the Treasury in Notre-Dame was unarguably the safest place for his mysterious oils – or at least, that's what everyone thought until they'd been stolen. Along with the new Tour Eiffel, the doctor's findings would have been at the heart of next year's Exposition Universelle. Since the Cabinet of Oils was stolen last year, the Exposition's organisers, not to mention every visitor to her roaster, spoke of little else.

Until today, a memory box tickled.

A nudge from Luc brought her back to the room, and she quickly made efforts to leave, but she could not. The doctor was towering over her, his arms arched around her like the claws of a hungry cat at its sparrow.

Nine | Neuf

"Bonjour, little one!" said Dr Le Chandelier. "You must be Piaf. How lovely."

Piaf shuddered. The doctor's words were mellow and sweet and took Piaf by surprise, but they clashed with his stance of authority. Gentle raindrops hissing on brazier-hot oil sizzled in her mind. She looked up and squinted. Did a smile accompany the doctor's words? She would not know, for a cloth mask covered the lower half of his face, its neatly tied strings dangling the length of his neck. They were swaying, almost begging her to pull at them.

Piaf squirmed where she sat and flashed a look at Luc, hoping it would direct the doctor's conversation that way. But it didn't work. She flapped an elbow towards her brother, then pointed. *He* was the patient.

The doctor's attention seemed firmly stuck on her.

"You poor little girl," said Dr Le Chandelier. "Your mother has only this second informed me of your sudden memory malfunction." Cornered on the bed, Piaf gulped as he adjusted the gauntlets of strange, thin rubber gloves that he wore. "So, you've decided you are living a year ahead of the rest of us?" He took her hand in his cold, rubbery glove and patted it.

"No, Doctor, that's wrong," Piaf said, but he ignored her. Piaf thought it very rude.

"Your memory deceives you," he said.

A determined box rattled and bounced to the top of the queue in Piaf's memory, and whatever was in it, it gave Piaf the urge to flee. Like he could sense it, the doctor ruffled her hair in an unexpected show of affection that made her flinch.

The doctor turned to the nurse. "As I thought, this affliction is contagious and must be contained. Psychosurgery, urgently, for the girl. For both of them, in fact. While I work on her, reconnect the boy to his Oxygène treatment," he said, pointing to the large bullet-shaped canister in the corner of the room that contained his renowned "fresher than fresh air". Long metal tubes and a leathery hood, which Luc was forced to wear as he slept, hung from a hook next to it like a sack of kittens.

"*Psychosurgery?*" repeated Luc, as the nurse wheeled the canister of Oxygène to his side. Piaf sensed Luc's worry. He was rubbing his chin again and his eyes were blinking like he was avoiding a determined shower of rain. Somewhere deep inside Luc's mind, he was recalling something he'd once learned, probably off-by-heart to "better himself", as he would often say. The flush on Luc's face from the asylum's stuffy heat suddenly drained.

"Psychosurgery is the removal of brain tissue," said Luc. "I must have read about it." He turned to the doctor, eyes bulging in disbelief. "You want to cut out some of our brains?"

"There, there, dear boy. It's a minor procedure, and I will take great care of you. The best." There was a short silence. "As though you were my own children. No more than a tickle, as I told your mother." He turned his head to address the nurse, and muttered, "*That* one would do good to control her emotions." His mask scrunched up like he'd smelled something bad.

"Pardon?" said Piaf. She saw oily sweat seeping into the creases of his mask.

Rattle! Piaf gulped as her impatient memory flagged another connection: that oily skin! That sweet-as-macarons voice! *Rattle!*

"YOU'RE THE STRANGER!" Piaf yelled and dipped left and right, dodging the swinging grasps of the doctor. She grabbed her brother and swooped off the far side of the bed.

The Oxygène with its metal tubes smashed to the floor between them with a *clang*, its large black canister spinning and hissing out a creamy, thick mist. It climbed upwards in a funnel, eerily slow, like a dying whirlwind.

"RESTRAIN THEM!" roared Dr Le Chandelier. He pounded his fist on a wall-mounted button only inches from the nurse's face, her shriek drowned out by an ear-piercing bell that smacked against walls throughout the asylum. As the doctor raced around the bed, Piaf and Luc slid beneath it. Discarded drawing pins pierced the thick skin of Piaf's knees.

"PIAF!" cried Luc. The doctor's hand was grasping under the bed. It found Luc's foot. Piaf grabbed

Luc's suitcase and shoved its hard corner against the doctor's arm until Luc was free. She rolled out from under the bed and swung her money bag in protective circles over her head like a chestnut on a string. Luc crouched behind her, his suitcase held as a shield.

The doctor lunged at Piaf. He grabbed her collar and held her at arm's length, her feet several inches from the floor. Piaf flapped like a bird in a bath, swinging her hands and money bag wildly at the doctor's face.

"Piaf! Luc!" Piaf saw the skirt of Madame Legrand's djellaba swaying at the door. "Doctor! WHAT ARE YOU DOING?"

"IT'S HIM!" Piaf yelled. "The man who tried to steal me!" Her fingers hooked the doctor's mask and she pulled it down. "Where is she – the girl you stole? And where's Bertrand Pufont?"

The man's nostrils flared, his skin purpled with rage. His face was pockmarked with fresh blisters.

Madame growled like a bear when her eyes and anger landed on the doctor's weeping sores. She grabbed a fistful of Piaf's coat and pulled at her until the coat ripped at the seams. "Burning chestnut flesh leaves its mark, *Doctor*," Madame spat, as Piaf's mother arrived at the door. "MARIE! Is this man a relation of yours?"

"A cousin?" added Piaf. She kicked the doctor's shins and twisted and turned and flapped every limb until she had no fight left in her.

"NO!" Maman collapsed into the arms of the nurse.

Dr Le Chandelier suddenly looked up and ducked like he was avoiding a greedy gull. So, Madame looked up, then Piaf, and her brother and mother too. The chubby fingers of the Oxygène canister's creamy mist bulged from a heavy cloud and threatened to float downwards. To avoid it, the doctor dropped Piaf to the floor but grabbed her matted hair and twisted it until she could not move. With his free hand, he urgently pushed his mask back on.

Piaf instinctively held her breath. The doctor was avoiding the Oxygène, his fresher than fresh air. *Why?* The swirling mist crept down and down and not once did he take his eyes off it. Piaf reached out and grabbed Madame's robe. She held on tight.

The doctor tickled the underside of the cloud of squirming mist as though it were the belly of a playful cat, but kept his head low. "Sincere apologies, Master Luc. I thought it was you who had what I needed." He laughed or seemed to choke a bit on his own words. "I regret I might have dug a little too deep in that interesting brain of yours. But it seems I had the wrong twin all along." The doctor yanked Piaf's head back and pointed to her forehead. "*That!* That memory of yours is all I need. It won't hurt, if you could, for once, stop moving." A jolt ran through Piaf as he flicked her as if to shake off an irritating fly.

"What is wrong with you?" barked Madame, "Why in hell do you want the memories of an eleven-year-old girl?"

"*Twelve,*" whispered Luc under his breath as he edged closer to the door.

Piaf flew over the universe of memories in her mind. What had she remembered that the doctor needed so desperately? "Tell me what you want to know. I will find it, I promise, and I will tell you! Just let me go!"

"I do not need your stupid *memories*, little girl. I need your *ability*," he spat. "I need it because…" He appeared to stop himself for a moment but then

71

looked up at the lowering, churning mist and nodded as though it had given him permission to say what else he wanted to say. Fire raged in his eyes. "The Exposition Universelle will be an exposition like no other. You are looking at the creator of something far, far greater than any stupid Cabinet of Oils. Far greater than that ugly Tour Eiffel. Greater than any gifted child I took; in fact, greater than any great mind to *ever* grace the stage at an Exposition." He tugged Piaf's hair tight, "You are coming with me."

With a stomp, Madame Legrand let out a mighty roar, forcing the doctor backwards against the wall. Piaf coughed out her breath as Madame grabbed her about her waist and yanked her free. Hairs wrapped around the doctor's gloves ripped from her scalp as she fell into the tangled folds of Madame's robe.

Maman cried out. Piaf crawled to her, desperate for her to squeeze the bedlam away.

The doctor and Madame faced each other.

"GET OUT OF MY WAY." He lunged at Piaf.

Madame blocked him and stood taller. Piaf saw her hand slowly clamp around Empress Josephine in a pocket hidden deep in her robe. She turned to Piaf and Luc. "Mes petites plumes! GO! FLY FREE!"

As Piaf and Luc ran for the door, Madame Legrand shrouded her head in her djellaba's wide hood before using her robe's folds to swirl and whip the creamy cloud down, smothering the room and all who stood in it.

Ten | Dix

The Winding Stairwell, Sainte-Chapelle, Île de la Cité, Paris

Tucked into the window ledge of a winding stairwell, Piaf felt chapel air, stale with the breath of the day's visitors, swoop against her face when the heavy doors of Sainte-Chapelle finally boomed shut for the night.

"He's gone," said Piaf, picturing the chapel's knight flattening his silk sash and straightening his beret as he always did before limping off home. The knight was a grouchy man. In fact, he complained as much as Piaf fidgeted, and she often wondered if, like her, he had good reason to. But she admired how he protected his precious chapel with a routine as impeccable as his white uniform – a routine Piaf, and once Luc, knew inside and out.

"The place is ours for the night," said Piaf. "We can hide here, at least until Madame and Maman get that doctor locked up." The memory of what the doctor had said about wanting her memory prodded like a pin in her mind. He'd said he had the "wrong twin all along". Wishing she had her squirrel button to twist, Piaf hugged her money bag hard, feeling the wooden chestnut inside press against her churning stomach, but it did little to stop the rattling memories in her mind. One danger-filled memory morphed into another: the doctor's hand was yanking her hair, like he was pulling her memory through her roots, and the scent of one hundred cherry berlingots suddenly swirled, both in the cramped space of her mind, and right here, in her narrow window ledge.

She scrambled down into the blue darkness of the chapel's winding stairwell and took a deep breath.

"The doctor wouldn't come after us, would he?" Piaf's wish slapped against the stone of the walls, but Luc did not reply. "Luc?" She quickly climbed several steps up to where he hid and saw the toe of his shoe jutting out from the wall. She punched it. "Luc! Whatever you do, do *not* fall asleep." It would take more than his list of twenty things to explain why he'd woken up tucked into a window ledge of Paris's most treasured chapel.

Folded like a letter too large for its envelope, Luc groaned. "I'm awake. Uncomfortable…" he said as he pulled at his too-short trouser legs, "but awake." He hunched his shoulders high, only to pull his shirt out from his waistband. "Agh, everything's too tight!" Piaf heard him hiss under his breath. Even in the darkness, she could see frustration widen his eyes and grit his teeth until he finally spat sewer words he'd once learned from Monsieur Auguste at Les Deux Magots. He then apologised, profusely, over and over.

"It's all right," said Piaf. Luc had cursed before, but she would never expect him to apologise to her, no more than she would expect him to apologise to himself. She was his twin. It was a sad thought that he might be trying to mask his angst out of politeness, like they had only just met. She gave him a pitiful smile. His suitcase from the asylum had held only one outfit, and the last time Luc wore it, he was a year younger. When it came to clothes for Piaf, anything would do, be it too big, stiff as sacks or scuffed to bits. Luc liked his clothes to be neat and tidy and, most of all, the perfect fit. Shoes that pinched or collars that scratched could bother him to the point of despair.

"You must feel rotten." Piaf noticed his shoulders drop an inch or so. "Your clothes are too small because they were put into your suitcase the day you lost your memory. *A year ago*," she added, still perplexed that Maman and Madame should challenge this fact. She hopped up and down the steps of the winding stairwell, careful to stick to the outer edge where the stone was widest. "Something's wrong with them, Luc. Madame even tried to convince me I was only eleven. They've gone mad."

Luc shifted his long legs and arms awkwardly, not used to their length. "Mother told me I was eleven too, even though the list said I was twelve. It confused her." He paused for a second, and asked, "Is she… is Mother *nice*?"

"Yes," said Piaf, and the boxes in her mind shuffled, offering warmer memories. "Maman would never, ever let anything bad happen to us. But she worries – she thinks I'm so small I might drown in a gutter." She fell short of telling Luc that he would always walk gutter-side because of it. After a short silence, she added, "We love Maman, just so you know."

"And Madame Legrand? I like how she smells."

Piaf smiled and nodded her agreement, "*Spices*. She buys sacks of strange ingredients from merchants at Port de la Bourdonnais." The buttery-yellow, powdered spices always seemed to coat Madame's Dutch clogs. "And she's Maman's friend – *best* friend," said Piaf. But for witnessing the joy and support they brought each other, she'd have lost all faith that such a thing as a best friend ever existed. How she wanted one. She sighed and it wobbled a bit, so she changed the subject. "You remember it now, don't you – this place?"

Luc shook his head.

A sadness squeezed Piaf's heart – this was the home of some of her best memories, best because they'd been created with Luc by her side. "*Anything?*"

"I know *of* Sainte-Chapelle," he said, rubbing his chin. "In fact, I know who built it, why it was built, its full history," Luc sighed, "but I don't remember ever being here before. It's cold."

For Piaf, constant fluttering always kept the cold at bay, but Luc was right. "I want to go home too, but that's the first place the doctor would look for us. Besides, this place is just like another home to us – every night, we'd sneak in here when we were done roasting. We'd hide while we waited for the knight to go home, and then count our chestnut money and pretend to be the King and Queen of Paris. Our secret," she smiled. It made Piaf think of Madame Legrand, queen of her own magnificent château. Madame spoke of it so often, but Piaf had never been. Maybe Madame was lonely, or cold, in such a big place and that's why she spent such long days at Pufont's. Luc shivered. "Come on," said Piaf. "I know something that will warm you up!"

With Luc on her tail, Piaf climbed up the winding steps on all fours until the darkness faded. She stood straighter when she reached the top, the joy of what she saw trickling like warm milk through her veins.

Eleven | Onze

The Upper Chapel, Sainte-Chapelle, Île de la Cité, Paris

"LOOK AT IT!" Like her eyes, Piaf's voice bounced around the magnificent chapel. It was lined with one stained-glass window after another, each narrow as a tree, and they stretched high for the heavens like a glittering, multi-coloured forest. At the other end, above an altar, was an enormous round window – the *rose*, each colourful petal a jewel, stunningly backlit by the night's full moon. The power of the chapel, made of so much glass it rendered its golden stone delicate, made Piaf feel infinitely tiny and powerful all at once – like she had the entire universe laid out before her.

Lost in its wonder, she sensed Luc reaching her side.

"It's so… *rich*," Luc gasped. His eyes followed the windows upward until they reached the vaulted roof, deep-sea blue and decorated with an explosion of gold stars.

Piaf laughed. "You're lucky you know, getting to see this place for the first time, *again*. Isn't it the best feeling?" She chuckled as she allowed that first-time joy to tickle her mind. Luc swung his arm over her shoulder and leaned on her. Piaf smiled. Luc really was back by her side. A tingle swirled inside her – their connection was deeper than a few lost memories, wasn't it? And now they were knee-deep in an adventure – a real game of hide and seek. This was going to make the *best* memories.

At least until Luc would fall asleep and forget it all.

"It's like a treasure chest," said Luc. He pointed up to one window where a plain-clothed, barefoot man was carrying a strange object in his hands. "See him? That's the king who built this place, so he had

85

somewhere to put all his treasures – mostly weird holy relics: dead saints' fingers and hair and magic teeth, old chalices of blood and stuff." He rubbed his hands together, like he was loving the gore of it all. "They kept all the relics here before they brought them to Notre-Dame."

"Oh!" said Piaf, pretending it was the first time she'd heard his lecture. She knew the story well, as did everyone in Paris – just over a year ago, and for the sake of tradition, an important man had dressed up like that king, and he carried Rapiditus's Cabinet of Oils from Sainte-Chapelle to Notre-Dame. Even those who thought "Saint" Rapiditus was a magician were happy to see the Cabinet of Oils treated like a holy relic. They made such a big deal of the ceremony, but Piaf thought the man looked silly.

Luc looked around him. "And I believe there is a real treasure chest somewhere—" A shrill whistle penetrated the glass from outside.

Piaf ducked behind Luc. "What was that?"

Luc nudged her and pointed towards a window.

Used to climbing chestnut trees, Piaf scrambled up the wall with ease, ten feet at least, to reach the bottom of the window. She braced her legs between the sides of two delicate stone arches and looked out. The scene out there, with its streetlights and cobbled stone, was entirely copper, it being tinted by a triangle of orange glass, and it would have been so pretty, only for the sight of a police officer.

He was yelling orders as he marched towards the grouchy knight and his friend – another knight. Piaf recognised this knight from Notre-Dame. He had looked after the Cabinet of Oils, and every photograph of it in *Le Petit Parisien* showed him standing on guard next to it. He had wept when it was stolen, according to talk at her roaster. She had labelled him kind – every evening, he would come to Sainte-Chapelle to help his limping friend, the grouchy knight, walk home. She liked how he would sometimes put on a limp too. Luc did that one time when she had twisted her ankle.

Piaf whiplashed out of her memories when the officer's whistle blew again.

The grouchy knight appeared to obey by standing on one leg and bending the other, his poorly one. On it, he balanced something.

"Sacré bleu!" said Piaf. She cupped her hands over her eyes. "The knight has your suitcase!"

"Told you we shouldn't've hidden it there," said Luc.

Piaf sighed – so maybe tucking it behind the chapel's wide-open door was not her wisest idea, but it was the only hiding place where Luc could get changed while the chapel emptied of visitors.

Piaf wiped her breath's fog from the window and looked out.

Using his sword, the kind knight plucked Luc's asylum gown out from the suitcase.

"Maybe the officer has come to tell us it's safe to go home, Luc. Maybe they've locked up the doc—"

The officer beckoned, ordering someone Piaf could not see to come. Only seconds passed before a tsunami of officers following Dr Le Chandelier rushed towards the knights. Piaf gulped. Facing the knights, the doctor held up two fingers, then raised one hand high before lowering it down several inches – tall and short; Luc and Piaf. He then held up a piece of paper, urging the knights to study it.

It was a photograph.

A photograph Piaf knew.

It was the one Madame Legrand had arranged as a special surprise to mark their twelfth birthday. The birthday she had since forgotten. It was the twins' first and only photograph, and Maman truly treasured it.

Piaf stopped breathing. Why on earth would Maman have given *that* to the doctor?

Piaf fought to put air back into her lungs.

"Maman is helping him," she said. She had whispered, but the words sliced the stale chapel air, rendering it stone cold.

Twelve | Douze

Piaf's memory hunted, finding the perfect word for what she was feeling: *betrayal*. She could not bear the hot mix of disbelief and sadness that swirled around her stomach like curdled milk. She shook, uncontrollably.

Maman was *not* having that doctor locked up. Maman was *not* making Piaf's world safe. Maman was *not* on their side.

With her bitten nails, Piaf clung onto the lead strips crisscrossing the window and felt her whole world sink. Horrid, painful memories of every friend who'd turned their back, tired of her tapping fingers, flapping hands or her counting out loud, and every time someone paid her no heed because of her size, stomped across her mind and lined up, ready to smother. But for the sound of Luc crying her name, she'd have drowned.

The doctor and his officers were coming in.

"HIDE!" roared Piaf. She jumped from a height, flapping her arms like a fledgling bird. She zig-zagged across the chapel hall, searching for cover. Though it was the most ornate place she'd ever been in, there was nowhere safe – beneath all that wonder, it was basically a rectangular room with low benches pushed up against each side where weary visitors could rest their legs and feast their eyes.

"The stairwell?"

"Too late," cried Luc. He swiped his finger in the air like he was turning the pages of a book. "The Grande Châsse! The Grande Châsse is somewhere in here!" He sped off towards the altar, stumbling as his tired legs failed to keep up the pace. "It's a *reliquary* – a huge treasure chest – the old king had it made to hold all his relics."

A whoosh of air climbed the stone stairwell and circled the hall as the front door of the floor below was thrown open. Along with it came a familiar voice, throbbing at Piaf's ears as it echoed throughout the chapel.

"SEARCH! EVERY INCH!"

Piaf gasped. "Dr Le Chandelier!"

There was a low, monotonous grumble of words. Piaf held her breath. *The grouchy knight.*

"OUT OF MY WAY! STUPID MAN!" came the doctor's voice, followed by an army of footsteps.

She reached the altar before her brother. She spun on the spot in search of the Grande Châsse. "Where is it? LUC! The Grande Châsse?"

Luc pointed up towards a small platform behind the altar. Piaf bounded up one of the wooden staircases that flanked either side. Upon an ornate silver table stood one simple candle, stamped with the crest of Sainte-Chapelle and overwhelmed by its dramatic holder, crafted with at least one hundred pieces. That was all, no Grande Châsse.

"LUC?"

Luc pointed at the silver table. "There! The table, only it's not a table, it's a reliquary – that's the Grande Châsse!" He ran a fingernail down from the Grande Châsse's top and paused when it met something several inches down – a hairline split in the silver. "Open it! Use your nails!" cried Luc.

"It's a lid!" said Piaf, in awe of something so skilfully

92

crafted that where its lid met its base was invisible. She clawed at it, Luc too, and how she wished she could use the tiny sharp hook at the end of Madame's Empress Josephine to lever it open!

Their efforts knocked over the candleholder.

Luc grabbed it and wedged its sharp base against the lid of the Grande Châsse until something budged. A gap, fingernail thick, was all he needed to get a good grip.

"Get in!"

Piaf peered into the Grande Châsse and her memory quickly told her it was the precise length and twice the height of Papa's coffin. In contrast to its shiny outside, etched with minuscule scenes and words in an alphabet long forgotten, the Grande Châsse was lined with a thick velvet so black, it appeared bottomless.

She sneezed when a waft of musty air puffed out. "Will we be able to breathe in there?"

Luc, struggling to keep its hinged lid open, had a fierceness in his eyes. "Either we get in, or get caught." He peered into the chest and groaned. "*Another* tight space."

Countless more footsteps powered across the

chapel's lower floor, their sound blown out of all proportion as it boomed up the stairwell. One by one, old wooden pews that had stood unmoved for hundreds of years creaked and crashed as they were shoved and tipped over.

Like mounting a horse, Piaf pulled herself up and threw her legs up and over the side of the Grande Châsse. Squatting inside, they held hands and looked at one another.

As Piaf took the deepest breath of her life, a beautiful memory strangely unfolded: she was with Luc. They were running, together, through the hot chestnut grove at the Jardin des Tuileries, celebrating the sight of the summer's first acid-green burrs. Like swooping birds, they jumped high to slap the largest chestnut leaves, each one flat as an open hand with five green fingers. They ran and slapped and then jumped highest of all, grabbed their knees mid-air and splashed into a deep, dark pond.

She smiled at Luc; his fear-altered face sadly uncomforted by any such memory.

I will remind him about it later.

The lid closed with a *thunk*.

Thirteen | Treize

The Grande Châsse, Sainte-Chapelle, Île de la Cité, Paris

Cramped inside the Grande Châsse, Piaf jolted when her brother grabbed her twitching hands and pressed them flat down onto the floor of the chest. She gasped; having lost her sight to the blackest of black, her sense of touch seemed to have doubled because, through her fingertips, something tickled and buzzed, stronger and stronger.

"What *is* that?" she whispered. Her words shook, her chest heaved.

"*Vibrations,*" explained Luc. "All the way from downstairs." He untangled his legs from hers and shuffled as far as he could into his end of the chest. "They're tearing the place apart looking for us, but listen…" He paused, so Piaf did too.

She gulped. "I can't hear a thing."

"Exactly. That's because this chest is completely soundproof – and it cost that mad king more to build than the chapel itself, all to hold a few weird relics. It's made to perfection." Piaf was sure he kissed his fingertips just as Monsieur Auguste of Les Deux Magots would do to a plate of frogs' legs. "As a matter of fact, it might be *too* perfect." His voice wobbled a bit. "It's also completely airtight…"

"I don't think I can breathe properly!" gasped Piaf. Sweat suddenly bubbled across her forehead, her underarms prickled, she felt like she was drowning in a bowl of thick soup. The sweet stench of one hundred cherry berlingots and musty velvet steamed about her. "And it's too dark! I can't tell if my eyes are open or closed." She blinked her lashes hard so she could feel them tickling her cheeks.

"It's all right!" said Luc, but Piaf knew that was a fib. "We *can* breathe – at least for a minute or so."

"A *minute?*" Piaf smacked her head off the chest's weighty lid. "Ow!"

"Quieten down!" said Luc. Piaf heard his hands hurriedly scanning the floor of the Grande Châsse and she instinctively did the same.

"What are we looking for?" asked Piaf. She swept her hands behind her, fearing she'd find a squishy heart or a pile of holy toenails. Relics on show in glass cabinets in Notre-Dame's Treasury were fascinating; relics swarming around her in a dark box were not. She touched something. "A dead finger!" Flapping her legs and balancing on her behind, she scrubbed her hands clean on the spongy black velvet that cushioned her in.

Luc smacked her feet from his face. "It's only the candle from out there." His breathing quickened, and so too did his words. "Hurry, give it here!"

Like hiding under bedcovers, the air suddenly felt hotter and tighter. Piaf's skin burned, her swollen lip throbbed. She wanted out. A clink and a metal-on-metal scraping sound filled her ears – was it her desperate lungs, begging? With her mouth open wide, she heaved and swallowed, but no air came. "Luc!" Her world, in all its blackness, spun and rattled.

A thread-thin white line appeared before her.

"Breathe," whispered Luc, "but not a sound." Between them, the thin silver base of the candlestick holder was now wedged into the Grande Châsse's lid, holding it open by little more than a hair's breadth.

Piaf pressed her lips and fingers against the line and drank in whispering air. Her entire body shook.

Suddenly, footsteps. They had a limped rhythm she knew: tick, *tock*, tick, *tock*. "The knight!" she warned. Louder and louder, the footsteps came; stronger and stronger, they buzzed. Piaf scrunched her eyes tight and tried with all her might to will the knight to go away with the power of her mind. In the silence, she pictured him surveying his chapel, searching, searching, tick, *tock*. The footsteps deepened as they moved from tile to wood. "He's coming up the stairs!" They were as good as caught. "It's the blasted candle, Luc!" Piaf snapped, quiet as she could. "You shouldn't have moved it – he's noticed it's gone!"

"It's not my fault," hissed Luc. "If I put it anywhere else out there, he'd have definitely seen it had been moved." His words stumbled over each other, "It's not so easy to see something that's not there—"

In panic, and probably sibling anger, Piaf slapped blindly for Luc's legs – with his trouser legs so short and his shins exposed, it was an accidental smack so loud, she pictured it shooting out the slit in the lid to meet their stalker's ears.

The footsteps stopped.

Tap, tap, tap; angry, impatient fingers of the knight drummed on the Grande Châsse's lid, directly overhead. The thin white line flickered.

Piaf twisted and squirmed like a cat in a sack until Luc pressed his hands down hard on her shoulders to steady her. She felt her hairs stand on end, drawn to the tapping noise like a magnet.

Piaf stilled.

They were in danger. Inside her mind, the bombardment of frightening memories began.

Goodness knows how long the knight stood there while nightmares flashed around her head. Worries and fears of old twisted her stomach: Papa's last breath; that time Maman's hair caught fire; when Luc forgot who she was. Even that stupid time her finger got stuck in the door kept playing over and over – every blasted horrible fright she ever got.

The knight slapped the lid of the Grande Châsse so hard, its sound grated in her sore ear and brought her back to the present with a jolt. More footsteps told her the knight was finally stepping away, and, like swimming back up to the surface, she counted to sixty before the chapel's front door slamming made her ears pop.

Piaf helped Luc push the lid of the Grande Châsse open until its extraordinary weight balanced it perfectly upright, and they sat there, gulping air into their lungs. With a groan, Luc unfolded himself like a newspaper. Piaf stood up beside him, her eyes only reaching a few inches above his elbow. She rose on her tiptoes, but her body shook and flapped like a frail and frightened bird.

"You all right?" asked Luc. Standing next to him, she could have sworn Luc bent his knees just then, enough to make her feel small, but not so tiny.

"Not totally," said Piaf. Blooms of blush spread across her cheeks. She turned a bit, and wiped tears that had tracked down her face and saturated her collar – tears that, only for their meeting cooler air, she wouldn't have known were there.

Luc smiled. "Me neither." He held out his hand before her. In the dim light of the chapel, it shook, more than her own. They were silent for a moment, but Piaf knew full well what was swirling around his head – for once, he didn't have to list the facts out loud:

They couldn't run to Maman for help.

They couldn't run to Madame, either. Crossing the city was too dangerous.

They couldn't even run to the police.

The doctor was the Parisian child snatcher, a man who had stolen twenty gifted children over the course of a year. He now had his eyes firmly set on Piaf.

As all hope sank, together, they sank back down into the Grande Châsse.

Luc squeezed Piaf's hand. "Please don't worry," he said. "Someone once told me there's no difference between feeling fear and feeling excitement – except how we interpret it." Piaf knew he was trying to keep her strong, but each word was weak, fragile as a feather.

"It was Madame Legrand who told you that," said Piaf. This fact should have added weight to his words, but, right now, it didn't feel like it. Piaf held her breath when Luc, exhausted and feeling the fear, dipped his head, and wept.

Piaf mooched her way closer and curled up beside him, snug as a bird in a nest. A memory gently tickled.

"There was this one time, Luc..." she began, determined not to miss a speck of detail as she transferred a memory into her brother's mind. "... in the middle of summer – not summer just gone, the one before that – you and me, in the Jardin des Tuileries, we pretended we were birds and jumped and smacked our wings off the leaves as we ran through the chestnut trees – *smash, swish, smash*..."

Piaf hadn't even reached the part where they'd dive-bombed into the deep, dark pond, when Luc began to snore. She knew, of course, he would later wake without a single memory of their day together.

She looked at him.

While hailstones began to hammer off the chapel's roof, Luc was sleeping peacefully in one end of the Grande Châsse, and he would wake up to a view of a rose window so spectacular that it would put the universe of stars to shame. She nodded; there was no better place for him, for wasn't *he* a treasure after all? Goodness knows what would become of them, with that doctor on their trail, but, in a finger-snap, she made a decision: she would rename that niggling, terrified feeling that had flipped and churned in her belly.

It wasn't *fear* she was feeling – it was *excitement*.

She smiled at her brother. "And do you know why it's exciting, Luc?" she whispered, almost daring him to wake. "It's exciting because we're in this together."

Fourteen | Quatorze

Piaf woke to blackbird song piercing through the rose window, announcing the imminent arrival of the sun. The last of the night's torrential rain died away and a queue of boxes whistled in her head, each bursting to share memories ignored: the stranger, the sinkhole and the girl's gifted chestnut; Madame and Maman's forgotten year; the doctor with his fresher than fresh air, and his intention to take Piaf's ability, and for what? Some great exhibition he planned for the Exposition Universelle? What had he done to the twenty stolen children? Poor Monsieur Pufont's grandson, Bertrand! Like carriages on the longest locomotive, the boxes went on and on. Piaf sighed. Her memories had unfinished business, and this was *their* time to be heard.

Quietly, she left the warmth of her sleeping brother's side and crawled over to the other end of the Grande Châsse, careful to keep her twitching limbs out of his way. For its heat as much as its light, she checked the candle was secure in its holder before placing it in the small space between them. She dug deep into her money bag for her roasting-cart matches.

She bit her lip when something stabbed beneath her thumbnail.

"The wooden chestnut," she whispered, her voice floating through the chapel's hall like morning mist.

The one impatient memory that had whistled of the chestnut, jostled to the front of the queue and displayed its contents with a relieved sigh. Piaf twitched as things re-shuffled in her mind, and she dropped the wooden chestnut onto the floor of the Grande Châsse. It landed with a *clop*.

"Oh," she said. Was it hollow?

Another memory – a small one, like a gentle footnote – politely tiptoed in her mind, so she listened: that *clop* she'd heard was just like the sound of Madame Legrand's set of Russian dolls on her workbench in Pufont's Button Bijouterie.

Clop went one doll's head as it closed snuggly upon another.

She smiled at the tickle of another connection forming in her mind: just like the dolls, there they both were, Luc and Piaf, hiding inside a treasure chest that was hiding inside a treasure chest of a chapel. And in her hands was another Russian doll, another hollow treasure chest, this time carved out of wood.

Could it have something hidden inside?

Piaf stretched her sleeves over her hands should its spikes hurt, and twisted the wooden chestnut; to the right, and to the left.

Click.

No Russian doll or sparkling jewels or tiny treasure lay inside.

Inside, lay the most delicate thing she had ever seen.

Piaf lit the candle and waited until its flame yawned itself tall, swaying gently in rhythm with Luc's quiet snores. She leaned into it, close enough to feel its heat, and rolled out the delicate prize that had waited patiently inside the wooden chestnut.

The wick's tip curled at her whispered words. "A *leaf?*"

106

She shook her head – *no*, it wasn't a leaf, but the mere ghost of one; its overcoat of green, or perhaps autumn brown, entirely stripped away. It was no bigger than the palm of her hand, and minuscule veins criss-crossed and curved around the leaf's see-through surface, holding precious its shape like an intricate web spun with the thinnest of gold thread.

"You're a leaf skeleton."

It was so tiny and fragile, and yet, even in these glorious surroundings, it was clearly the most beautiful thing she had ever seen. Getting lost in its lines, she remained still, still as Madame Legrand's mice, until quick as the candle's flicker, Luc was awake.

Fifteen | Quinze

"Don't fret, please don't fret," said Piaf, but her words were not only aimed at Luc as he yawned himself awake. They were also aimed at herself. Nerves worsened her twitching muscles and flapping hands; while Luc had slept in the Grande Châsse, she'd thought about how best to bring his lost mind up to speed, but goodness knows how he'd likely react – waking up day after day, memoryless, in an asylum was one thing. Waking up in a priceless reliquary without a clue who he was, was another thing entirely.

She quickly returned the leaf skeleton to its wooden burr and began to hum Maman's lullaby that would be familiar to Luc. She handed him a list – a new list of twenty things, just like the one pinned to his bedside table back in the asylum. It was written on crumpled paper found in the creases of her money bag – the writing was messier than Maman's, but Luc would not remember that.

Piaf picked at her swollen lip, and Luc studied the list.

With one side of his curls flattened and pressed against his cheek, he suddenly stretched and smiled. "You forgot the bit that says you are shorter than me."

"What did you say?" Piaf jumped to her feet, ignoring the chestnut as it rolled from her lap and tipped the candle, sending miniature fireworks into the space between them.

"I can remember!" said Luc.

Piaf squealed – a spontaneous cry of joy so high-pitched it could break glass, just like the opera singer at the last Parisian Exposition, then witnessed from her pram. "You can? You can remember?" She threw her arms around her brother.

"Whoa! Wait! I remember *yesterday*. Just yesterday." He pulled at his tight collar.

Piaf sat back on her knees and frowned. "Oh."

"But it's clear as day." Luc stood up in the Grande Châsse and turned slowly in a circle. "The asylum; the

109

drawing pins on the ground…" He pointed to where he could see them in his mind's eye, "The smell of cabbage soup and soap; my scratchy blanket; you, filthy, at the door, and your sinkhole; Mother – over there in her chair." He licked his lips as though he'd tasted sugar for the very first time.

"The doctor?"

Luc nodded. "The doctor. The *child-snatching* doctor who wants to butcher our brains. And you, so sure Mother and Madame had forgotten the last year. I remember *every* detail about yesterday, Piaf."

"But you can't remember anything that happened *before* yesterday?" asked Piaf. How odd.

"The earliest thing I can remember is taking off a leather hood thing, then I saw Mother's list. That was just before you arrived." He spun his finger, just as Madame had done when she'd described Piaf. He climbed out of the Grande Châsse and walked over to the edge of the balcony, almost in a daze.

A memory box tickled. "The hood, Luc, do you remember the doctor's remedy – his *Oxygène?*" asked Piaf, wriggling her whole body just as it had done as it squirmed down from its creamy cloud in Luc's room. "He called it his 'fresher than fresh air'… but if it was so fresh, why was the doctor avoiding it? Did you notice that – how he was ducking his head?" She climbed out of the Grande Châsse and walked over to Luc's side. They both leaned on the rich wood of the banister and stared down upon the altar. "Dr Le Chandelier made you breathe that Oxygène anytime you slept. The hood left a mark on your chin—"

Luc raised a hand to his face. "And then I'd wake up, having forgotten everything that had happened before I slept."

Piaf gasped. She turned and pointed to the empty Grande Châsse. "You didn't wear the hood last night—"

"And now I can remember!" finished Luc.

They stood staring at one another. "His Oxygène *made* you forget!"

"He poisoned me! The doctor poisoned me! That was not Oxygène he gave me." Luc flapped the air between them with Piaf's handwritten list. "*This* is Oxygène. *A clear, colourless diatomic gas with the formula* O_2," he recited from some textbook stored somewhere in his brain. He swung his arms out wide and leapt down the small wooden staircase, whipping

111

up the cool chapel air. "*Clear* and *colourless*! As in see-through, like the air we breathe," he shouted up to her. "Not thick and squirmy. Not white!"

A memory box in Piaf's mind promptly flipped its lid and its contents uncurled like a scroll. "Yesterday, in the asylum, as soon as the doctor saw his Oxygène over our heads, he told us everything – *dévoiler un secret*, as they say," said Piaf. "He confessed it all, Luc, because he thought everyone would forget what he was saying as soon as we breathed his Oxygène. He said he messed with your brain too much. That he had the wrong twin all along. And he didn't stop there – you heard him, he even confessed to stealing other children—"

"We must get help with this, Piaf. This is too big," said Luc, his voice serious and urgent. He marched off towards the spiral stairwell, like he had somewhere to go.

"We're on our own," said Piaf, and her hollow words climbed up the chapel's forest of windows, louder and louder, until Luc stopped in his tracks. No one would take their word against the word of a world-renowned doctor. "*Evidence*, Luc. That's what we need." The train of boxes in her mind hammered

112

and clattered like they had something to say. "There must be something that we can use to prove he's dangerous... I think there might be a memory that could prove it," Piaf rapped all fingers against her head, "but it's all too loud, so loud I can't hear it. Clatter! Clatter! Clatter!"

Luc raced up the small wooden stairs two steps at a time and came to a sudden stop inches from Piaf's face. He studied the furrows on her brow like they were a maths sum that needed solving. "How do you eat an elephant?"

Piaf squinted. Had he gone mad too?

"You eat it one tiny bit at a time – that's how. Pick one – one memory. Start somewhere."

"All right. *The girl with the crooked nose*," said Piaf. She shuddered when the memory box of the girl chained to the doctor swung open its lid impatiently. "If we can find out who she is, and prove she's been stolen just like Bertrand Pufont, maybe the police will believe us. *Evidence*." Piaf marched back to the Grande Châsse, now lit up by a slice of morning sunlight. "She gave me the wooden chestnut, but that's not all. Look..." She picked up the wooden burr and twisted it open. She held it and its leaf skeleton high enough for the sunrise's debut light to fizzle through it. "Maybe it's a clue."

Luc was by her side, quick sharp. Instinctively knowing that even a strong breath could blow the delicate leaf away, he carefully reached in and pinched it free of its wooden bed. He gasped at its beauty.

Piaf stared at the leaf skeleton in Luc's hand, its minuscule veins clearer now that the sun had begun to rise. Something about them looked familiar. "She gave me this for a reason, Luc." The memory of the girl with the crooked nose had no sooner tipped its hat by sealing its lid tight and duly returning to its resting place when, in its place, stood another box: a box of maps.

"Oh! It's a map!" said Piaf, "The girl is trying to lead us to her!"

"It's Paris!" cried Luc.

Piaf squinted her eyes and focused on the tiny lines. "That map has nothing to do with Paris," said Piaf. It didn't have a river, not to mention a *looping* river large enough to have its own island like Île de la Cité. "I could draw a map of this city with my eyes closed, and *that* is not it." Having remembered every street she'd ever set foot on, maps of Paris spread from her memory box like tiny grass roots.

"It *is* Paris!" Luc ran his little finger along a tiny, straight line. "That could be the Champs-Élysées." Piaf raised her eyebrows. It was true, but the road on the leaf was far narrower. "And that bit there, that looks like the Jardin de Tuileries. And that bit."

Piaf had to agree – there were similarities. It was like the map was a twin of Paris, but not an identical one; just like Piaf and her brother, they were different, but somehow the same. The box of maps in Piaf's mind suddenly hopped when the memory of falling down the sinkhole stomped. She had seen a tunnel down there, much like a narrow road, one that stretched out as long as Rue du Dragon until darkness with strange golden eyes stole its end. A penny, and a sense of dread, dropped.

"It *is* a map of Paris," realised Piaf, "but not *this* Paris." She whistled loudly as Madame as she took in the vastness of the city held in such a small leaf. "Paris has a twin sister; one city filled with boutiques and sparkling lights and life, up here for all to see." She waved her hands towards the beauty and confidence of Sainte-Chapelle. "The other city hidden, all filthy

115

and ignored." She looked down and scraped sinkhole dirt from her trousers. Somehow her own words began to make her feel sad. "The girl with the crooked nose is down there, beneath our feet. *Underground*."

Excitement, it's excitement, a memory box swiftly reminded her; *not fear*.

Piaf felt a buzz, deep inside; Paris's underground twin might have been hidden, filthy and ignored, but it was an underground city that had yet to be explored. She quickly snubbed out the candle's flame, gathered it up and the new list of twenty things, and shoved the lot into her bag. Finally, she held out the wooden burr for Luc to place the leaf back in its home.

"Are you ready? We need to go back to the sinkhole." She shuddered, and not only for the memory of the long, dank tunnels with their swarming eyes – she shuddered at the thought of brazenly walking overground, halfway across Paris's busy sixth arrondissement to get to the sinkhole in the first place. "We need to start there."

"Or there?" said Luc. He pinched the end of the leaf skeleton's stalk and held it high, using the rose window's glow as a backlight.

Piaf flicked a look at the leaf and back to Luc.

Using his little finger, he carefully placed it dead centre where a star symbol, so tiny Piaf had to squint, was set in an octagon. "That's where Notre-Dame is. And it practically says, *Start Here*."

Sixteen | Seize

Boulevard du Palais, Île de la Cité, Paris

With mouthfuls of warm and stolen baguette, Piaf and Luc's getaway from the patisserie across the road from Sainte-Chapelle launched at speed. Not only were they being hunted by the doctor, but they had now swiped bread from under the nose of an old baker – an action Piaf knew would remain in a box labelled *guilt* for ever. They were *fugitives* now, according to Luc, so it was a price she had to pay.

Luc was always the better runner, but Piaf quickly caught up with him. She pulled him into the shadow of a parked horse and carriage where so many jostling

118

legs would keep them hidden. As she caught her breath, a flurry of excitement danced inside and she searched Luc's face, wondering if he was feeling it too. They were on an adventure; an adventure to find evidence that would put that doctor behind bars. Then it would lead them to the stolen children, and it would force that evil man to fix whatever he had done to Luc's memory. Evidence would do all that – evidence in the shape of a girl with a crooked nose. And, according to the little star on the leaf skeleton, their adventure would bring them underground at the great cathedral of Notre-Dame, once the home of Rapiditus's stolen Cabinet of Oils.

Luc was panting like a dog in July. His hands leaned heavily on his thighs.

"Are you all right?" asked Piaf, but knew he wasn't; how weak he had become from so much time spent lying in bed.

Luc nodded, ripped a bit of bread with his teeth and blamed his tight shoes.

He needed a bit of time. Piaf stood on her tiptoes and pointed towards a tall grey building, just a stone's throw on. "See there? That's the back entrance of Paris's police headquarters." She snatched a gnarled horsewhip from the carriage's holder and drew a large teardrop shape in flattened horse manure. Luc stopped chewing his bread and retched.

"This is Île de la Cité, and we are here." Piaf bore a hole with the whip, then drew a rectangle inside her teardrop island. "The police headquarters takes up the whole block – it goes around the corner onto the laneway until it meets Rue de la Cité." She drew a wide avenue that split the river's island from top to bottom.

"On that end of the avenue is Hôtel-Dieu." She tapped the manure flat at one end of Rue de la Cité and drew an X further along the same avenue, leaving the police headquarters in between. "And that's where we need to get to – Notre-Dame – where the star is on the leaf map. But we can't run," she said, hoping that would bring her brother some relief. "We can't look like thieves or fugitives, not here anyway. We need to look like we're fetching… I don't know, thread or spice for Madame Legrand or something." An image of Madame's enormous pyramid of colourful spools of thread danced across her mind.

Pulling at the armpits of his sweaty shirt, Luc nodded and said, "Good thinking." Piaf's shoulders straightened. Luc always led the way, but when he seemed to wait for her to make the next move, she walked on at a casual pace, ahead of him, like she supposed a fugitive on an adventure should do.

They turned the corner onto the small lane.

Leading the way, she felt strange – knowing she should be worried, having the doctor and the police hunting them down – but, somehow, for once, she felt free. Like she had flown a nest. She even began to skip along. But, suddenly closed in by tall buildings, big problems and giant risks, she felt small again and found herself instinctively slowing down. She let Luc pass her, and she walked, small and in his shadow. Like normal.

Despite her still-swollen lip, she chewed frantically on her baguette as she looked around. It was early morning but the lane that led to the wide road was eerily quiet, but for the click and whistle of starlings. As they approached the end of it, where the buildings lowered from serious offices to small cafés and boutiques, the noise level rose – a deep humming sound, with odd bursts of shouting, or was it singing? It was distant – like it was coming from the far end of Rue de la Cité.

"Is that coming from Notre-Dame—OH!" Piaf ran to catch up with Luc and tugged on his elbow.

She pointed to a lamppost.

Her eye jumped to the shops lining the far side of the lane. Overnight, posters had been haphazardly slicked to every surface. Each was stamped with the serious mark of *Préfecture de Police de Paris*, declaring the twins dangerous, and her a thief – a thief who had stolen her ill brother. The pinch in her stomach changed, its thin layer of excitement and freedom quickly dissolving, leaving only an ache of something that felt like proper fear.

This adventure of theirs was no longer an adventure – what had she been *thinking*?

Using her baguette, Piaf hid her face from a single passing carriage to her left and ripped the poster from the lamppost. She dragged her brother to her side and slid into the narrow alcove at the corner, where the cobbled lane met the long and wide Rue de la Cité.

She wanted to kick herself.

"We've been too careless, Luc!" cried Piaf. "Walking down the road so casually like that!"

"And stealing bread?" added Luc. "A stupid risk." Piaf cowered a bit – it had been her idea, but it was the only way to stop the loud rumbling in her stomach, not to mention her mind. "We've been asking for trouble." He looked at her with a question etched deep in his face – was she always so reckless?

The answer, of course, was *never*. She usually followed in the safety of his lead. She knew her place. Goodness knows what had come over her, stealing and skipping along like that. "Did anyone see us?" She looked left and right.

Though Paris's police headquarters stood directly behind them, countless carriages and their horses appeared to have been abandoned along the lane in a less than orderly fashion. Across the wide avenue to their left was the Hôtel-Dieu, with its row after row of arches sitting pretty above its unspoken asylum. Being sandwiched between the two horrid buildings, where *she* had suggested they go, was possibly the worst place to be.

Piaf sat down on her haunches, tight as a chick in an egg, and stretched out the poster on the damp ground before her. Any guilt she had felt for putting them there was quickly stamped out by something else.

"A *thief?*" she read. She took an angry bite of bread. "That doctor is a LIAR! Oh…" She used the last of her baguette as a pointer, '… and we're a *great danger to the city*." Thick block letters told the world they were WANTED, and below that was the photograph the officers had shown to the grouchy knight – the photograph Maman treasured.

Piaf stopped chewing.

She couldn't help but ask again, and this time out loud. "Why is Maman helping the doctor?" If Luc answered, she did not hear. As with all unanswered questions, this one was floating about her mind having nowhere to settle. It floated and floated, looping around the small memory box where Maman and Madame had seemed to forget a whole year, until it floated some more and came to rest against a box oozing with the doctor's remedy – his precious Oxygène. Like Maman was proud of it and him.

It left chill bumps on Piaf's skin. She scratched at and rubbed her arms. They not only needed to convince the police of the doctor's doings, they needed to convince one of his greatest admirers, too – Maman.

While Luc studied the leaf map for any hint of

where in Notre-Dame they would find a way down to the Underground, four boxes lined up in Piaf's mind:

Family. A box for Piaf, and one each for Maman, Luc and dear Papa.

Like all her memory boxes, they seemed to be linked together, almost holding hands. But the link to Papa's box had entirely broken. It was shattered for ever the day Papa died. And the links between the first three were now kinked and twisted, *strained*. There was no way on this earth Piaf would let those links break. She would repair them.

Piaf found herself racing onwards towards Notre-Dame. As the humming and singing rose louder and louder, so too did her determination; they needed to find their evidence – the girl with the crooked nose – and find her quick.

Seventeen | Dix-sept

Notre-Dame Cathedral,
Île de la Cité, Paris

Piaf swore the river's small island of Île de la Cité was tilting to one side – what appeared to be half the population of the city had gathered at the island's great cathedral of Notre-Dame. Suddenly, the fresh October air was gone, replaced with the sweet scent of breakfast crêpes being churned out from street-stalls. Haunting music mingled with out-of-sync prayers, flags and candles were waved in the air, colourful bunting trailed from lamppost to lamppost. It reminded Piaf of a carnival Maman once spoke of, but, before she got lost in that story of acrobats and three-legged children, she jittered and quivered to keep her focus on where they needed to go: *underground*.

She sensed Luc's urge to back away from the edge of the crowd – habit perhaps, since Maman had always warned him not to lose his sister in one. He anxiously rolled the wooden chestnut burr in his hands.

Wondering why such a crowd had gathered, Piaf pointed towards the thick of it. "Come on, we should get in there." When Luc took another step back, she tipped her head towards a shuffling line of officers on horseback further down Rue de la Cité. "Look – over there." At the island's bridge, officers were filtering people like one giant sieve, just as they had done last year when that man dressed up like the old king in Sainte-Chapelle's window to carry Rapiditus's Cabinet of Oils to Notre-Dame. She'd missed Luc badly that day – it was so busy, Madame even had to step in and roll newspaper cones for her. But this was different. "Luc – I think they're stopping people leaving the island."

Luc gasped, "Are they are searching for us?"

"That's why we need to camouflage," said Piaf,

attempting to sound just like him, always matter-of-fact. "And the crowd will help us do that," she explained, remembering the hours she'd spent searching through a sack of glossy chestnuts for her favourite one; the one with the heart-shaped white patch. Unique as it was, it was almost impossible to find.

"What the... Piaf!" Luc dragged her back with a bite of shock in his voice. He pointed towards the end of the line of officers.

"Maman!"

There she was, standing next to an officer. The officer was pointing back towards Sainte-Chapelle and Maman was nodding, *agreeing*, with whatever it was the man was saying. She was wearing the same clothes as the day before. Piaf scanned the area for Madame Legrand – was she there, too? Maybe they could run to her?

Luc nudged Piaf.

At the other end of the line of officers, one of the horses was now standing out of line, and it carried a large officer. He was hunched forward, squinting in their direction. Piaf slammed shut the fresh memory box of Maman helping the doctor, grabbed her brother's tight shirt and dragged him deeper and deeper into the crowd.

Like a flock of birds, the crowd pulled them forward, fast and then slow, tossing them left and right and twirling them into a tight whirlpool until they stood cramped, facing one another.

"Don't lose me!" Piaf could not help but shout. "Don't lose me!" Having usually avoided crowds because of Maman's fear, she clung desperately to her brother's shirt. But, as soon as Luc stared down at her, she let go and stood on her tiptoes, wishing she could take back her panic. Smaller than everyone, she forced her chin high and her mouth shut. She stared up at the circle of strangers surrounding them. Was that man beside Luc mimicking her? He was stretching high, craning his neck.

No, they were all at it.

"What are they looking at?"

"A miracle, I guess," said Luc, standing tall on his tiptoes too. His eyes were wide open, a strange smile on his lips. Like he would do on sight of the highest chestnut burrs, Luc instinctively bent his knee for Piaf to climb up.

In a split second, Piaf was sitting on his shoulders.

Feeling high as a bird on a treetop, she followed the crowd's stares until her line of sight came to a sudden, solid stop: she was looking at the daunting twin towers of Notre-Dame. The cathedral's statues were highlighted like a gallery of kings – someone was using one of those spotlights she had seen at the last Parisian Exposition. Other than that, all was normal.

"What is it?" she yelled down to Luc. "What am I looking for?" Her eyes jumped from the row of statues to the intricately carved stone arches, from the massive round window all the way up to her favourite bit – the ugly stone gargoyles and chimeras; each creature so petite, yet so fierce. Gasps swam up as more people joined the crowd, buffering the twins in from behind. She could feel her heart thumping; whatever was going on, it was going to be good. Perhaps the statues were moving? Or, better still, had they finally found the stolen Cabinet of Oils? Was *that* what this was all about?

A man to her left pointed up. "BLANC GLORIEUX! A MIRACLE!"

Luc patted her leg. "The cathedral, Piaf! It's white!"

"Well, I wouldn't say it's *white*. It's yellow, like butter," said Piaf. She admired it for a second or two – the builders had done a good job cleaning the stone over the last year; it was practically black before. Scrubbing towards a deadline as special as the Exposition Universelle was hard going, according to the dust-covered builders at her roasting cart, but while all that work might have worked up a good appetite for chestnuts, it fell well short of a miracle. Maman digging up a carrot that wore Papa's lost wedding ring as a belt: now *that* was a miracle.

Piaf scanned the crowd until her eye fell on one familiar head in the distance – Monsieur Auguste of Les Deux Magots on her corner at Rue du Dragon! What was he doing there? And why on earth was he blessing himself? Like her Papa, Monsieur Auguste was a solid supporter of the revolutionaries who fought to remove the church from its pedestal one hundred years ago. He'd even plastered his café's walls with the *saint-less* calendar they'd used back in the day.

"It's a miracle!" another voice drifted up. It was a man, and he was smiling at her – perhaps because she didn't seem so small up there on Luc's shoulders.

"Excusez-moi, but *no*," replied Piaf. "The workmen worked hard, but there's nothing miraculous about it. Haven't they been cleaning the cathedral all year?" Piaf felt Luc squeeze her leg – perhaps they couldn't hear her from down there. She cupped her hands around her mouth for volume. "IT'S NOT A MIRACLE."

The man turned to face her, square. His head was almost level with hers. "Allez!" he said, but quick as a flash he turned his attention to Luc. "Bring your little brother home."

This was why she hated making conversation. It was not the little brother bit that had bothered her – that was a common mistake people made. It was the fact that he now chose to ignore her, like she was nothing.

"She's a girl," was all Luc said.

"Clearly, whatever she is, she is blind, for she cannot see one of our Miracles Parisiens when faced with it. So many miracles!" He raised his hands to the sky and prayed a bit before declaring, "This is très spécial. Yesterday, we wake up, and it is like new. It has been reborn."

Piaf recoiled when his strange words triggered memory boxes in her mind, each racing to recite even stranger things customers had said at her roaster only the day before – before the stranger had arrived. One woman swore her kitten grew to twice its size overnight. A man had woken in a strange house but with all his possessions. And she'd overheard another say St Nicholas had come early, leaving him two new wheels on his bicycle and a new coat of paint on his front door.

It was as though they had all— "Oh, mon Dieu!" A thought had hit her, fast as a steam engine.

Piaf scrambled her way down. "It couldn't be!" She looked at Luc and gulped. "Don't you see, Luc? They *think* a miracle has happened. They *think* the cathedral turned from black to white overnight! But it didn't – it took months." She found herself staring at faces in the crowd like exhibits in one of those forbidden freakshows up by Montmartre. "Maman and Madame are not the only ones who have forgotten the last year! *Everyone* has forgotten!" The world had gone mad. "EVERYONE!"

Luc scratched at his head. "Everyone, except you."

Eighteen | Dix-huit

Piaf turned in a tight circle, staring, wondering, waiting for the enormity of it all to shrink to a size she could comprehend. What on earth was going on?

Packed in by the crowd, she imagined she was flying high above it, the vastness of it filling her bird's eye view. So many people. "Look at them, Luc. They truly have forgotten. I thought maybe someone had found Rapiditus's stolen Cabinet of Oils – but, no…"

A woman turned and stared at her so sternly it urged Luc to place a protective arm around Piaf. Piaf stared back. The woman was very small too, for her age, her back hunched so badly it made her smaller still. In solidarity, Piaf offered a little smile, but the old woman kissed the cross on her rosary beads and repeated Piaf's words.

"Saint Rapiditus's *stolen* Cabinet of Oils!" she sang, over and over. Piaf thought it odd. Heads turned, whispers turned to shouts. As though a stone had been thrown in water, Piaf's "news" of the stolen Cabinet of Oils spread outwards through the crowd.

"I think they had forgotten that too," said Luc.

Piaf grimaced. Luc was right. The Cabinet of Oils was stolen nearly a year ago, almost to the day. It was no ordinary treasure – it was a cabinet of ancient magic and mystery yet to be unravelled, something believed to be so powerful that next year's Exposition was being built around it. But now visitors from near and far would have to make do with the Tour Eiffel instead. "Sorry," she offered to several shocked faces.

People started to pull at Piaf, digging for more information. As fears of their precious Cabinet of Oils being stolen rose, Piaf and Luc dipped low and pushed forward. "We need to get out of here," cried Piaf. "We need to go underground!" She kept her eyes down, almost wishing for the ground to give way like before. They were tossed and dragged with the current until, suddenly, everyone stilled.

Piaf spun around and looked up. Up into the faces of an officer and a knight.

Clamped by the crowd, Piaf shuddered; her mind filled with a tower of boxes ready to shout of times she'd gotten herself into trouble. The officer swung his hands out wide, stopping the expanding bulge of people behind him in its tracks. The knight to his side expelled a puff of garlicky breath. It was the kind knight again, friend of the grouchy one in Sainte-Chapelle; the knight who had been charged with protecting Notre-Dame's Treasury and all that lay in it.

"The Cabinet of Oils of Saint Rapiditus, maschiettò?" cried the knight, his Italian accent almost beyond comprehension. Piaf was not sure if he was asking a question or stating a fact, but his face was as white as his cloak, sweat already bubbled and clinging to the band of his black beret.

"It was stolen," Piaf began to explain.

The officer growled. Piaf gulped.

"I didn't steal it!" It was best to get that out there in case anyone should think otherwise. Nobody listened. "I have never stolen anything in my life," she declared and physically ducked when her memory swung a warm baguette. "I'm not a *proper* thief! Not like Dr Le Chandelier. He's a *real* thief. He stole my brother's memory. He even stole the missing children! All twenty of them, I reckon! And now he's trying to steal me—" Piaf stopped when Luc elbowed her. It did all sound utterly batty, especially to a crowd who had no recollection of the year in which the children went missing. "I did NOT steal it!"

"She didn't steal it," said Luc.

The knight nudged the officer to one side. Piaf jumped backwards, treading on toes, when the knight reached for his sword. "By the Order of the Holy Sepulchre, I demand you confess! What did you *not* steal?"

"STAND BACK!" The officer's whistle clinked off his teeth as he roared. He stepped in front of the knight. "This is not a matter for your Order, it is a matter for the Préfecture de Police de Paris!" His voice came from his boots.

Luc gulped. "Piaf, I don't think a missing Cabinet of Oils is on this officer's mind." He pointed to a familiar poster crumpled in the officer's hand.

"THE ASYLUM TWINS!" roared several spectators. Fingers, like gladiator spears, pointed at Piaf and Luc.

The crowd heaved as several knights slipped through it like ghosts.

"Knight Angelo," one said to the kind knight, panting. "Cabinet XXVII, home of the treasured Cabinet of Oils of Saint Rapiditus from the Basilica of Our Lady of the Thorn in Évron – Notre-Dame's inaugural requisition of this century – is empty. The Cabinet of Oils is gone."

Piaf's eyes jumped from the knight to the officer.

"WHERE ARE THEY?" came the doctor's voice, so loud Piaf was sure the cathedral, which towered above them, held its breath.

"The doctor!" Piaf flittered in circles, not sure which way to run. They had to get away.

The officer blew his whistle and yelled something about ropes. Then arms! So many arms! They plucked at her and pinched her until she was firmly trapped. The officer, unable to tame Piaf's flapping arms, placed his hand on top of her head and pushed down. She was stuck. There was a screech as another officer bulldozed his way through, clearing the way for the doctor. He'd shouldered Luc. As Piaf watched her brother crumple to the ground, she saw the chestnut burr drop from his hand. She swiped it closer with her foot and bit the forearm that crossed her neck. Flittering like a bird caught in a finger-cage, she squeezed free of grasping hands.

She swung low for the burr, and ran.

She didn't even look to see if Luc was behind her. She smashed through the crowd. "LUC!" she cried, over and over. "THIS WAY! Follow me!" she roared, scooting and swishing past anyone in her way, zigzagging like a hunted bird through thorny brambles.

Was he there? Was Luc following? Fear grabbed her breath; the sun burst through a cloud, blinding her. Not far from the cathedral's front entrance, she stopped dead.

She'd felt something, inside her mind, go *clunk*.

Suddenly, she felt warmth across her shoulders, like an angel's wings folding around her. Though she was breathless, she felt safe, and still.

Are you listening? whispered her memory, wrapping its wings tighter into a hug. *Trust me and spin.*

Piaf looked down. On the ground, she saw a plaque. No bigger than her roasting pan, the octagon of bronze was set neatly into the pavestones. It was dotted with countless shiny coins, each loaded with wishes and hopes of the day's passers-by.

"*Le Point Zéro de Paris*," she said, skating her foot over the coins. She was standing at the centre point of the great city, a spot always thronged with sightseers, history lovers and optimists. She pushed the coins to one side and stared at the plaque's centrepiece: a bold, brass star. A memory so recent it had yet to be filed in its box, tickled and told her she was standing at the centre point of something else:

"The star on the map," she said. A picture of the leaf skeleton floated through the narrow tunnels and alleyways of her mind, like a feather on a breeze.

So, spin, her memory said, its whisper blowing the leaf further still.

Piaf dropped to her knees; she thumped and bashed and clawed at the plaque, trying to dig her small fingers into the gaps around it, wishing for Empress Josephine's tiny hook. "Let me in!" she cried.

Spin, her memory said again, and there, in her mind, she saw the girl with the crooked nose, raising one leg and spinning as far as her chain would allow.

So that's what Piaf did: like an awkward ballerina, she raised one leg and spun on the spot. The plaque spun anti-clockwise with her and the star beneath the ball of her foot sank down an inch until it, too, *clunked*.

She took one last glance around her before, once again, the ground opened up and swallowed her whole.

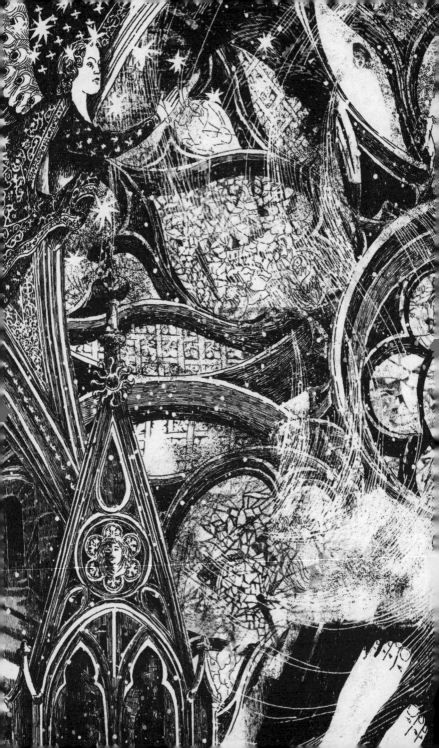

Underground

One city, filled with boutiques, sparkling lights and life,
the other, hidden, filthy, and ignored.
So different and yet so alike.
Paris's twin.

Nineteen | Dix-neuf

Tagine-Pot Hollow,
Beneath Notre-Dame, Paris

Piaf braced herself for a hard landing. Coins rained down around her, and her toes were only feet from solid ground when she was yanked to a stop, mid-air.

"AGH!" Dangling, Piaf thrashed her arms and legs, stubbing her bare toes on the slanted stone walls that surrounded her. Someone from above had reached through the hole and grabbed the strap of her bag, its cherry berlingot scent slapping her face as she was set off into a wild spin. She twisted her neck to look up, saw glimpses of an arm, then knuckles.

"LET GO!" She jammed the spikey chestnut burr into them.

"Gotch— OUCH!"

Piaf hit the ground and rolled like an egg to one side, sneezing wildly when a cloud of stone-dust puffed into the air. A bundle crashed down beside her, legs and arms poking out in odd directions. She picked up the burr, ready to defend, but the circle of light that came from above shone down on a tight shirt and bare bellybutton she instantly recognised. Coins spun to a halt either side of it, almost silently, before they were swallowed by powdery dust.

"LUC!"

Luc groaned and rolled onto his side where the light beamed down, directly into his eye. A shadow crossed it. He jumped to his feet and scrambled for the plaque. "Quick, Piaf, close the hole!" He slapped the plaque into her chest, knocking her back against something hard and jagged. Piaf heaved as he wrapped his arm around her waist and flung her up onto his shoulders.

A roar boomed down the hole, soon followed by an arm.

"The doctor!" cried Luc.

With the plaque clamped to her chest, Piaf clambered higher and higher until she was standing on her brother's shoulders, her bare toes curling and clasping just as they would do on a chestnut tree branch. The metal plaque was heavy, and, with his weak legs, Luc did well to keep balance as Piaf swung wildly, bashing her elbows off loose rough rock either side. She smashed the metal plaque sideways against the doctor's arm and did it again and again until he wrenched his hand back up, his thick silver ring taking a clump of her hair with it.

"HIGHER!" Piaf yelled at Luc as she struggled to push up, dust and chips of stone scratching at her eyes. She stretched herself taller than she ever did before and the plaque twisted back into place with its *clunk*.

They were thrown into complete darkness.

A muffled threat came from above; "I will hunt you down," said the doctor. He thumped the plaque hard with each word. "I WILL finish what I have started, and I WILL get you."

Piaf instantly lost her balance and crouched down, clinging to her brother's head like a startled cat and praying the doctor did not see her spin like the girl to gain entry. Like her, Luc jerked side-to-side seeking out even a dot of light. She heard his breathing, quick and shallow, just like it had been in the Grande Châsse.

When the doctor's attempts to open the plaque finally ceased, Piaf slid down Luc's side and urgently rummaged in her bag. Her fingers found her roasting-cart matches and the Sainte-Chapelle candle, and a few seconds later their surroundings flickered into view.

They shuffled in a circle as one.

They were inside a buried stone hollow, as wide as it was tall, with pick-axe scars where hard stone had been gouged out. The space was the same shape as one of Madame's tagine pots of delicious spicy wet meats she'd kindly bring Maman: like an upside-down funnel, the space was round and wide at the bottom, leading up to a short neck with a hole at its top, now plugged by the plaque. Like spider's legs, eight narrow tunnels spread out in all directions from where they stood.

Golden eyes from Piaf's sinkhole fall swarmed the tunnels in her mind and she turned on the spot, waiting for more to appear.

"What *is* this place?" asked Luc. His voice wobbled

152

like a bowl of gelée. "Do you really think we'll find the girl down here?"

Piaf nodded. She was certain; why else would the girl with the crooked nose have given her the map? A memory box rattled; the girl had ghostly white skin, like it had rarely seen the light of day, and her eyelids were heavy, probably sore from the stone-dust. Recalling the countless tunnels and passageways intricately carved out of the leaf skeleton, Piaf said, "It's certainly big enough to keep her hidden."

"Big enough to keep all twenty children hidden," said Luc. They both held the thought tight.

Piaf looked down at Luc's quivering hand when he grabbed her wrist, urging her to hold the candle closer to the tunnels. Not unlike the sinkhole tunnels, the stone was warm, buttery-yellow, and neatly excavated. It instantly reminded Piaf of the freshly cleaned stone of Notre-Dame, and she began to wonder if she was looking at the birthplace of the cathedral itself.

Piaf moved the candle closer still.

Etched into the limestone above one arch was a skull with crossbones.

"A warning!" they said in tandem. They both gulped and looked back up towards the way out. Something stomped on the plaque, sending down streamers of chipped stone like cheeky sparks of hot oil from their roaster.

Their eyes and the candle's light jumped from tunnel to tunnel. Each sloped downwards from where they stood, some quite dramatically so. Etched out of flat rock just inside the entrance to one tunnel to Piaf's left, she saw letters. The letters had not been urgently hacked out; they were etched with serifs and perfect finger-spacing between each, like newspaper headlines.

"*Crossroads des Morts?*"

"Crossroads of the dead," explained Luc. "We're not going that way." Inside the entrance of another tunnel opposite, hung one polished tile for each letter: *Rue de la Cité*, just like the street above it, and next to that, *Salleverte 1763*, this time so thinly scratched out like it had been etched by Empress Josephine herself.

Piaf chewed on her swollen lip. Which way to go?

She held the candle down towards the ground and scurried around Luc's legs. "There it is." She held up the chestnut burr and blew dust from its spikes, sending the candle into a panicky flutter. Sitting down on her haunches, she twisted the candle into the dirt until it was propped up before her feet. Urgently, she twisted open the burr and tossed the shell into her bag.

She carefully unfurled the map and held it close to the flame.

"WHOA!" cried Luc, as his head jerked backwards. "LOOK!"

The slanted tagine-pot roof filled with a distorted shadow cast from the leaf skeleton. A map, of gigantic proportions and infinite detail appeared across the buttery stone like an enormous lace parasol.

Piaf whistled. "De toute beauté!" she cried, the same way Madame Legrand would say it when she'd sewn the last fine button onto a garment. The dancing flame vibrated the shadow's intricate maze of fine lines like a windswept spider's web. Her eyes darted side-to-side, not knowing where to settle, just like the first time she'd seen the forest of windows in Sainte-Chapelle.

"Piaf! Hold it still… THERE! See it?" Luc pointed up towards the brass plaque. "There's the star symbol."

Piaf's eye darted from the minuscule star on the leaf to its shadow that now flickered on the underside of the plaque overhead. Just like the tunnels surrounding Piaf, eight wriggling lines burst outward from the star's shadow like gnarly oak branches. Off these were countless more branches and even smaller ones off them again – they filled the hollow's walls with the finest cracks, just like she'd seen one time on a blue egg. It had signalled the hatching of a robin, tip-tapping it from the inside with its tiny beak, impatient to see the world outside. Another image of something cracked began to develop so she wriggled a bit to stop herself from getting lost in tunnels, this time in her mind.

"Give it here," said Luc as the map bounced back and forth in Piaf's fluttery hands. He held the leaf's stalk as firm and steady as his nerves would allow. The map was better, but still trembled.

Piaf stared up in awe of the map and its tunnels. She braced her hands either side of one archway that was without signage and breathed in cold, damp air. A swirl of excitement tickled her tummy. "If we find her, we can prove to the police what the doctor really is." A sad box rattled. "And Maman, we can prove it to Maman too." She cracked all her knuckles and then flittered from tunnel to tunnel, one for each word:

"WHERE ARE YOU, GIRL WITH THE CROOKED NOSE?"

A loud chorus of echoes bounced back. Piaf covered her ears with her hands. "Start somewhere – that's what you said, Luc! Pick a tunnel!" She missed his words but saw him point at the shadow as it folded around her stomach. There was another symbol, far smaller than the star.

Piaf bent her neck down and stood as still as she dared. "A tree?" It had all the appearance of a thick trunk, the tiniest of scrapings along it like rough bark. Hairy lines sprung out from its top and its bottom too. "Are they roots?"

"Yes," said Luc.

Piaf's pointed finger was already twisting and turning its way from the tree symbol back towards the shadow's star. Several kinks and wavy lines later, the path thickened as it met the star where they stood. "It's the biggest tunnel from here," she said, comparing it to the seven others. She turned in a circle until she found the largest arch. "That way!"

"Mon Dieu! Maybe not," said Luc, staring at the skull and crossbones above its entrance.

A scraping sound drowned him out.

"The plaque!" cried Piaf, "It's spinning!" She glared at it as the shadow map was swept away. She plucked the leaf from Luc's quivering hand. Instantly, it curled itself around her finger like a bandage, snug and tight.

"Careful!" Luc warned, "It's so, so fragile."

"It's stronger than you think," said Piaf. She grabbed the candle and off they crept, down the deepest, darkest tunnel.

Twenty | Vingt

Tunnel of the Tree, Beneath Île de la Cité, Paris

A witch's cauldron sprang to mind; slugs and putrid dead mice, fingers of green slime, furry balls of fungus and skeletons of things long dead surrounded her. Unlike the sinkhole's dry, coarse tunnel beneath Rue du Dragon, the dampness here soaked deep into her bones; a dampness that stank like the River Seine at the end of a very hot day.

Piaf sighed. Countless times she'd pulled Luc to a halt and questioned if they should turn back. And countless times she'd stubbed her toes and ripped her clothing on jagged rocks as she made her way through knee-high black water. Scratches burned and muscles ached. She peered down on the flame of the candle she gripped tightly in her hand to cast a wish – a wish that the girl with the crooked nose would simply appear – but she suddenly felt a burning flicker of unease in her stomach.

"Luc, we need to stop." She turned to face him so hurriedly the candle hissed. "I think this is what they call the point of no return," she said, staring at the struggling flame. In the two hours they had been walking, crawling, sliding down steep bits, and squirming through collapsed tunnels, the candle had burned down to half its height. Two hours searching, and there was no sign of the girl.

She held up the candle. "Do we keep going? If we go any further, we won't have enough light to get back." Paris was known for its grandeur: from the new Tour Eiffel – a giant even at half its unfinished height – to the majesty of Notre-Dame and the Arc de Triomphe; from the endless galleries of the Louvre to the white domes of Sacré-Cœur, each big as a moon. Paris was huge. It was only now that Piaf began to *really* grasp the enormity of the city's underground twin.

For a moment, Luc stared at the candle. "Sacré

bleu, you are right." He sighed and came a little closer, scooting his muddy shoes along the thin ridges that flanked either side of the tunnel, just above the water.

Piaf had not fussed when he'd decided to walk that way, despite it slowing them down. It was bad enough wearing shoes too tight, he had explained, but walking in tight, *wet* shoes was simply too much to bear. She felt sorry for him, his fear of uncomfortable clothes worsened by walking with his legs spread wide and his neck bent.

Piaf held up her finger where the leaf skeleton clung on tight. "Should we check the map?"

Luc dropped several small stones he'd held in his hands, used to fire at rats lounging on his tracks, and pointed to the candle. "Give it here, then." He held the candle while Piaf unfurled the leaf. She held it close to the flame, filling the tunnel with its lacey shadow.

Luc quickly nodded towards the route they had chosen as it danced on the wall. "Where are we? We must be nearly at the tree by now."

Piaf stopped chewing at her lip, splashing her frozen legs and flicking her dusty hair from her eyes. The map came into better focus as she wound down her fluttering and stood still. She dived into her memory, reversed a couple of hours before fast-forwarding her way back to where they stood. She reported back to Luc as her memory reached points of note, from the skull and bones archway, through wide and narrow ever-deepening tunnels, past the tight bit where she cut her knee; the hole where Luc did his business, and then the wall with the tally-marks. They'd reminded her of the scratches on Madame's Empress Josephine. Oh, to be back with Madame, sitting on her workbench in Pufont's Button Bijouterie while she snipped at her hair.

"After the tally-marks, we turned right," she continued, and watched as Luc followed the map's trail with his finger. "We took the second left that went upwards, before it went back down again, into water – this bit." Her stomach's rumbles finally closed the lid on her memory box and brought her fully back to Luc. "I'm hungry."

She followed Luc's gaze, firmly glued to an area midway along one zigzag on the map's shadow just above her head. "Are we *there*?" she asked. She reached up and pressed her finger against a smooth rock beyond the shadow. She was surprised she could reach it.

Luc nodded. The distance to the tree seemed less than the distance travelled – they had enough candle to get there, wherever "there" might be.

"So, we keep going?" said Piaf.

"All right. If that's what you think we should do," said Luc.

His response slapped her nerves – making a decision like that weighed a tonne! Far, far too much for someone like her! She wasn't even sure the old Luc would've said such a thing.

"I wasn't *suggesting* we keep going, Luc, I was *asking* you— Luc?" Luc's attention was elsewhere. He had taken hold of Piaf's wrist to steady the leaf.

Only an inch further along on the map there was a kink in the line; a dot the size of a sugar grain sat alongside the tunnel. Only visible when the leaf was held perfectly still, it was so tiny, it must have been made by the sharpest point of the tiniest pin. "What *is* that?" he asked.

Together, they turned and stared down the tunnel and waited as if the walls themselves would utter the answer.

Twenty-one | Vingt-et-un

"It's tiny, so it's probably nothing," said Luc as his pupils darted trying to cling to the shivering dot on the map.

Piaf knew he meant nothing by his words, but something about them made her want to punch him – a proper scrap like they would often have, fighting over who would crack open the largest burrs in the Jardin des Tuileries. "There's only one way to find out if this *tiny* dot is *nothing*," she said, secretly wishing it were something huge. Luc picked up on her grated words and he blushed, so she allowed the leaf to curl back around her finger and forced herself to take a deep breath. She plodded on, sloshing through the water until, finally, the tunnel climbed its way to a

164

dusty dry level. The powdered stone clumped and tickled between her toes.

Luc jumped down from the ridges and stretched his back so straight its crack echoed back up the tunnel. Relief seemed to spread through him, float through the air, and on to Piaf. "That's better?" she checked.

"Better."

Up ahead was a sharp bend. While Luc stalled to adjust his clothes, Piaf moved on, the candle held before her. She peered around the bend, but quickly moved the candle behind her back and looked again.

"I see light!" she called back to Luc before being drawn towards it. Further along, to the left, an alcove – like a wide shelf – had been carved into the wall at hip height. It was the length and width of her bed back home and its height would easily have accommodated the drawing of a sparrow she'd once cut from the front page of *Le Petit Parisien*. She'd hung it over her bed. She loved how the tiny bird was printed so huge it looked powerful – like a giant. Piaf did well to shake the image away and focused on the bed of rock before her.

A single, crunchy leaf and shards of broken glass sat in its centre.

Swiping them away with her sleeve, she climbed in. She lay down and looked up. In its flat stone ceiling, she saw a narrow, round hollow, not so different to a chimney's flue. It was less than the width of a lamppost, and led to a pinprick of flickering daylight, too far up to measure.

As her tired muscles sank onto the slab of rock, a draught, like a cold cup of water, poured down upon her. Fresh air. She placed the candle down beside her, its flame fighting hard against the breeze. She stilled and was suddenly at Fontaine Saint-Sulpice once again, her head cocked back, allowing its water to cool her scalp on Paris's hottest day in years.

Luc reached her side and shook her. "What is it?"

"A hole!" She sat up and pushed her arm up into it. "It goes all the way up to the outside. I suppose it's there to let the air in. We are way, way down."

The candle gave up its fight against the draught, and died.

"Piaf!" cried Luc.

"It's all right! We can still see!" A gasp slipped out when Luc's face appeared before her – with the warmth of the candle gone, he appeared grey as a ghost. Shadows blue as bruises circled his tired eyes. Poor Luc. Piaf patted the surface of the flat stone next to her. "I think the candle could do with a rest for a while. Sit."

Exhausted, Luc awkwardly climbed in and, as they sat cross-legged facing each other, he sniffed the air between them. "What is that smell?" He crinkled his nose.

"Fresh air—"

"No. It's like… soap, only *sticky*."

"Oh," said Piaf. "Like one hundred cherry berlingots? It's the doctor." She pulled her bag's strap over her shoulder and held it up to Luc. Four oily fingerprints caught his eye, but something else caught Piaf's. Somehow, tiny feathers of steam, only clearer than the air itself, seemed to rise from the strap. Before she could say something, one seemed to hook Luc's nose and he bent down for a deep sniff.

His face creased with lines. He jolted, like he was saving himself from a fall. "I… I remember something. A… *memory*. A proper one." He sniffed hard again but then threw the strap back into Piaf's hands. "That day you found me by the tree… did you see anyone else?

167

Someone a bit like a … was it a *ghost*?" He gulped. "It must have been a ghost – it was floating, just off the ground." He squinted as he dragged the remnants of his only memory to the surface, like he'd woken from a dream.

"Smell it again!" Piaf held it close to his nose. "Go on – smell it again!"

"I really don't think I want to," he said nervously, but Piaf could tell by the tip of his tongue sticking out between his lips that curiosity was at war with his nerves. She handed him the strap.

Luc sniffed the strap tentatively and flinched when the sickly-sweet scent tickled his nose. Fear suddenly bleached his skin. He spoke fast. "I could hardly see her – the ghost – she was there, and there was blood, then she was gone! And I couldn't breathe, and I couldn't move... something was on my face." He slapped and pulled at the skin on his cheeks like it was swarming with insects. His breathing quickened and his eyes filled with tears. Patchy as the strange memory was, seeing Luc relive it made Piaf shudder. She knew what that was like, being haunted by bad memories.

Piaf quickly took back the strap and hugged Luc

as hard as she could. With every breath he took, she told him everything was all right, and only when his heaving chest weakened and his tears stopped, did she gently lift his chin and whisper, "Look up. It's like looking at a star."

Inches from Luc's curly hair, the circle of dim light poured down the narrow shaft between them. He stared up and his pale face lit up, inky blue. His eyelids flickered, like he was searching for something to drown out the horrid memory for ever, like eating something pleasant after something rotten. He found that something hidden in the corner of his mind where songs, poems and times-tables lived.

"What are stars, but snowflakes," he began,
"Too afraid to fall from the greatest of all heights.
They remain; twinkling, twisting, flickering, flittering.
Then one, so brave, unhooks itself to float down. It lands beside me,
My precious, flickering, flittering star."

Silence followed while they both digested his words.

It was not a poem Piaf had heard before, and it appeared to wrap a warm, snuggly blanket around

Luc. He looked soothed, and he yawned. After a minute or so, he lay down and rested his head on her lap. He squirmed himself into comfort, closed his eyes and said, "I think I wrote that about you."

Piaf's mouth hung open. He wrote that poem about *her*? She hadn't a notion that she could mean something so... so *big* to anyone. She looked at Luc and never before had she felt so *together* with her brother – like the rest of the world had disappeared and the universe was all theirs, just the two of them. The words she wanted to say back to him seemed to get lost, and poured as tears instead. She did well to cup them in her hand before they fell upon him as he drifted into sleep. A welcome and warm feeling began to buzz inside, so much so she feared Luc would feel it vibrating through her every muscle. To quieten herself, she ran her fingers up and down the strap of her bag, just how Maman would sharpen her knife on a strap of leather, willing the feathery steam to rise from the doctor's oily prints again. Just as one rose, there was a thud of rock on rock, close enough to know that she'd heard *it* rather than its echo. She gasped.

They were not alone.

Twenty-two | Vingt-deux

"Luc!" Piaf whispered. She shook his shoulder, "Wake up! I heard something!"

As Luc raised his head, Piaf leaned out of the alcove and peered down the pitch-black tunnel. A small light was floating, gently, in the darkness, how far away it was hard to say. It reminded her of a dandelion seed, carried by a breeze.

Before fear could grip her, a special memory leapfrogged over a rising army of danger-filled ones: that time she'd found her lost chestnut – the one with the white heart – hidden beneath the spoons in the cutlery drawer. Lost and then found.

"The most important lost things are found like this, Luc – when you least expect it," she whispered. Pins and needles surged through her veins as she climbed her way out of the alcove. She cleared her throat, cupped her hand around her lips and said in a most gentle voice, "Is that you, girl with the crooked nose?"

The light froze.

Piaf tiptoed forward and crouched down as though she were tempting a stray kitten with the corner of a tasty Croque Monsieur. "It's me, the Chestnut Roaster." She flashed a look back at Luc and felt her cheeks redden as though she'd been caught red-handed with something that didn't belong to her. She'd roasted as many chestnuts as Luc, but why did he always wear the label of Chestnut Roaster better? Sometimes, it was subtle – the quick nod of thanks directed at him, despite her doing the roasting. Most other times, less subtle.

The light juddered, then zipped away like a shooting star.

"She's gone."

Without saying another word, Piaf urgently searched her bag for matches and relit the candle. Before the flame had properly taken hold, she hurried down the tunnel. Finding the girl was more than a game of hide and seek. Finding her meant proving to Maman and the world that Dr Le Chandelier was a child snatcher – a dangerous man who had poisoned her brother, robbing him of his memory with his so-called Oxygène. He had to be stopped, and to do that, they had to find their evidence: the girl.

"Arrêtez! Stop!" Piaf cried, over and over, as she ran as fast as the candle's flame would allow, and hoped her words, or their echo, would reach the girl's ears. She ran and ran and ran.

Skidding to a halt at a crossroads in a wide part of the tunnel, Piaf spun around, holding the candle out before her. She tried to hold her breath and it took a second for her to realise it wasn't her own heart she could hear tapping. The sound was rattling towards her, its echo like a Parisian mademoiselle in high heels. *Clack, clack, clack.* Maman had made her try on a pair once, just for fun, and she swore never again.

"Ouch!" Hot candlewax rolled across her fingers, snapping her attention back. She quickly straightened the candle.

Luc reached her side, panting. "It's coming from down there," he said and pointed down a tunnel to their right. It was a narrower tunnel, like a country lane off a busy city road. The ceiling was lower, the ground uneven, the walls made entirely of sculpted mud rather than chiselled stone. As they walked, they climbed, up and up, the effort burning the muscles in their thighs. Large rocks too big to remove were left in situ, forcing them to dip and curve their bodies around them.

A couple of minutes in, the temperature rose sharply as did the volume of tapping. Piaf's lungs fought harder to fill; flakes of dried mud scratched in her throat and stung her eyes. Inch by inch, the walls closed in, until large, muscular tree-roots twisted around stones like knots of snakes.

"Roots, Luc – we're at the tree symbol."

The tapping came louder and louder.

And then, around one more tight bend, she saw something she would never forget. The tunnel was straight as a die and its carved-out mud walls were pockmarked with small, cube-shaped indents, each no taller than the length of her forefinger and an inch or two from the next. She likened them to the tiny pigeonholes she'd seen in the new post office on Rue du Louvre. However, instead of postage stamps, each hole contained a tiny wooden carving.

"An owl," she said holding the candle up close to one. "A bucket. A little wheelbarrow."

Luc gently moved her hand upwards, shining the light on row after row that went up to the ceiling of the tunnel just like the bookshelf in Maman's bedroom. Piaf's arm swooped down the other side and that wall, as far as the eye could see, was also adorned with wooden carvings. "There must be hundreds," she whispered. It was as though every object in the living world above had been carved and recorded for an underground museum. The details of each piece, their precise lines and their perfect curves, were all exquisite.

They reminded her of her lost squirrel button. Such skill. They reminded her of the leaf skeleton too.

Luc nudged her.

"Girl with the crooked nose?" Piaf called, gently. She took a few steps forward, past the tiny flowerpot, the smallest ball of yarn, the miniature cup and saucer, and soon she was walking full throttle past countless wooden objects. "It's me. The Chestnut Roaster," she said every ten steps or so and, each time, glanced sideways at her brother. He didn't seem to mind. She finally neared a tight bend to the left.

"Bonjour?" said Piaf, a shake in her voice. "It is me, the Chestnut Roaster," she said again. The tapping stopped. She ducked behind her brother and they shuffled around the corner, every muscle tense.

Behind a curtain of finger-thin, dangling roots, the cramped passageway opened out to a large, square hollow, similar in size to her bedroom. It brought the tunnel to a dead end. Everything in it was coated with the same yellow dust both Luc and she were bathed in. The floor was covered in a carpet of wood-shavings, bulging higher in parts like ripples in the sea. It was like a nest. The low ceiling dipped towards the far side of the room; tree roots hung freely like sprouts on an old potato. A worktable had been carved straight out of the muddy walls to her left, at least twenty tiny tools and chunks of wood tossed about it.

It was a mess.

Her eyes darted to the right. Larger shelves held wooden plates, cups, and stick things with feathered edges that Piaf could only presume were small hair or toothbrushes. Oil-lamps hung from sticks on opposite ends of the back wall, hazy warm light bursting from each. A cosy box of more wood shavings lay in one corner – a bed, perhaps – above it hung etchings, one filled with what appeared to be shooting stars which reminded her of the ceiling of Sainte-Chapelle.

Despite the mess, it was the homeliest, most lived-in place Piaf had ever seen. The smell of fresh wood, just like a freshly opened chestnut burr, was divine.

Amongst it all, sitting on a large flat rock in the centre of the room, was a boy. He was smartly dressed, yet coated in yellow dust but for a small patch below his bottom lip where his tongue had been before Piaf and Luc shattered his deep concentration.

Luc said nothing, so, in the safety of her brother's shadow, she blew out the candle and said, "It is nice to finally meet you, Bertrand Pufont, best Button Maker in Paris."

Twenty-three | Vingt-trois

The Museum of Objects,
Beneath Le Jardin du Luxembourg, Paris

The boy felt his hammer slip from his hand – the hammer he'd proudly fashioned from a stone and root-wood, found as near to the Overground as he would dare go. In the other hand, he tightly clutched his best small chisel. The piece of wood he'd held between his knees slid down, bunching his woollen socks as it fell before landing on his toe. He didn't yell.

A survivor – a tall and thin boy, with a shock of curly hair – stood before him. What a sight to see! Another survivor had survived! He was not the only one! The tall boy looked just like how he'd imagined another survivor might look, with some minor differences. It was in the details: the way his shoulders sloped; he had a small mouth which hung open like a fish he'd once carved; and he had a red mark across his chin. His trousers stopped several inches above his ankles and his toes looked bunched in his shoes – perhaps Doctor did not provide for this boy as well as he had provided for him. Something flapped and flittered like angel's wings behind the tall boy. To get a better view, he shifted on his stone seat and doing so prompted a barefoot girl survivor to appear.

She was small. Curiously, she seemed to guard herself by staying tucked behind the tall boy's arm, but it was clear by the look in her eye that she was in charge. He could also tell by her ragged clothes, torn fingernails, and matted hair that she was a hard worker, and he wondered if she had tunnelled both of them here by mistake. Did Doctor know of them?

"Can I call you Bertie?" the girl finally said, her voice light but quivering; not from nerves, but from the storm that seemed to travel through her from her head to her toes; *twitch, twitch, twitch*. She wore a huge smile, and she was wonderful and not at all what he'd imagined.

He stood up, suddenly aware of the wood shavings clinging to his clothing like mushrooms on damp earth. "You can call me whatever you like, mademoiselle." He did not have need for a name. At least, not until now. They stood in a triangle, staring at one another. Where had they come from, this tall boy and small girl? Another arrondissement? Did Doctor know? "I think you are lost," he said. "You are now in the sixth arrondissement." To be clear, he pointed to his wall map, carved from narrow strips of wood, and detailing every inch of his district, including new features of his own making. It hung over his bed and next to his best work: his etching of falling stars.

As one, the two survivors turned and stared at the map. The girl pointed to something wrapped around her finger – a dead autumn leaf?

His stomach rumbled, loudly. "Boy, girl, you must leave – Doctor is due to come with my food, any moment now. If he finds you here, he might be upset after all he has done for us." Why on earth would they want to risk upsetting Doctor? "Go home to your own arrondissements, s'il vous plaît."

The girl's face twisted, like she didn't understand his words.

"He said *doctor*," whispered the tall boy.

The girl put down her candle and took a step towards him. Her hands spoke wildly before she did. "We haven't met before, but you do know me – I'm the Chestnut Roaster from Rue du Dragon. I buy your buttons from your grandfather's shop." She held out her arm and fiddled with its sleeve. Its cuff was missing, but she pointed to where it ought to be. "Madame Legrand sews them into my cuff."

There was no button to see, but what she had said made his fingers tremble and his hungry stomach flip.

"Rue du Dragon? You can't be from Rue du Dragon. It is also in the sixth arrondissement and the sixth belongs to me. Strictly one survivor in my district – that is the rule." The Doctor had warned him so. "You will breathe too much of my air."

The tall boy was chewing on his lip and squinting, and then he said, "You can't remember your life, can you?" The girl looked at the tall boy, puzzled.

He frowned. He was going to explain to the two survivors how he was lucky his memory was all he'd lost when so many others lost so much more. He was going to explain how he was blessed that Doctor was doing his best to fix him. He was going to explain how they should be grateful that they were in this boat too – they were all survivors – and he was going to tell them that upsetting Doctor by coming to this region, his sixth arrondissement, was a very strange way of showing it. He was going to say it all, once he'd found the courage, but the girl spoke again.

"Of course!" the girl cried, excitement lightening her words. "You made this, didn't you?" she asked. She tapped the side of her head and seemed to pay gratitude – to whom? Her mind? She unpeeled the dead autumn leaf from around her finger. It was see-through. "A girl gave it to me... yesterday, up there." She looked up, as though she were speaking of the Overground. "You must know her! Is she down here?" She handed over the leaf.

He secured Doctor's old monocle against his eye. Carved out of the leaf's surface, he could see all twenty arrondissements of the Underground with tunnels less than a hair's breadth wide. Though the carving was as exact and delicate as his own work, so much so it could have been made by his own hand, he knew for certain he had not made it – he had no idea what lay beyond his own region. He shook his head; the girl frowned.

"No one else could carve something so fine," she said. Gosh.

"It led us down here to you," said the tall boy.

"And it will lead us back up there. *Home.*" The girl flapped her arm as if to usher him out. "Back up to your grandfather."

Surely, they were speaking nonsense. "You can't go up to the Overground. The air broke when the stars fell." He nodded towards his etching of shooting stars. The tall boy quickly approached it and began rubbing his chin. "Doctor told me all about it," he said to the tall boy. He put on a kind voice, and quoted the man himself: "*The scene was truly awful for never did rain fall much thicker—*"

"… *than the meteors that fell towards the earth,*" finished the tall boy.

"Oh!" said the boy, "You know Doctor's words?" They *did* know him! Why hadn't Doctor mentioned these survivors before?

The tall boy turned and stared at him, "Your 'doctor' didn't tell me those words – it's an old quote I read in a book one time. And I've seen a drawing just like yours in the Bibliothèque Nationale. It's the Great Leonid Meteor Storm of 1833. That's over fifty years ago…"

"…and there is nothing wrong up there now," said the girl, picking up where the tall boy finished so smoothly, he wondered if they were twins. "No stars fell," she insisted. "The air is fresh!" She stepped even closer and placed a hand on his shoulder. He wanted it to stay there, it felt so warm and soft – a touch he didn't know he needed. "Your doctor has been lying to you," she said, sweetly. "He stole you, and it's time to go home to your grandfather."

No stars? Grandfather? Stole? What *were* they saying?

"I don't understand you," he said to the tall boy and the girl, but felt the fool. He sensed embarrassment crawling up his neck, but then a thought struck him, and he raised his chisel in triumph, "Oh! Maybe Doctor's great plan actually worked – it fixed the air! Is that what you mean?" He glanced at his collection of small glass medicine bottles, stacked up like a trophy on a shelf over his worktable.

The girl and boy frowned, together. Perhaps they *were* twins.

"And we only did it the once!" he smiled. "Does Doctor know? He will be so pleased when he hears— Shh! Listen…" A distant humming was reverberating through the tunnels. "I think he comes now! Doctor!—"

The girl shouted something about cherry berlingots and her words made the tall boy apologise before lunging towards him and clasping cold hands around his face. The doctor's monocle fell from his eye as the girl held the strap of her bag to his nose.

"Smell it!" she ordered.

And things were never the same again.

Twenty-four | Vingt-quatre

Piaf jostled where she stood and flapped her hands so hard it burned her wrists. An army of danger-filled memories threatened to overwhelm as Dr Le Chandelier approached the Button Maker's dead-end nest. They were trapped. She threw the strap of her bag back over her shoulder, the smell of one hundred cherry berlingots hitting her like a wet leaf. She stared at the boy, waiting. Had the smell worked? It *had* brought a memory back to Luc. Three against one might give them a fighting chance. Her heart pounded.

The boy suddenly burst into tears. He hugged his own shoulders with his hands, the saddest yet happiest smile spread across his cheeks, and a tiny cry like that of a newly hatched chick filled the room and flew straight into Piaf's heart.

"It worked?" checked Luc, urgently, his eyes wide. "Can he remember?"

"Grandpère?" the boy said.

Piaf nodded. She put her hand on his arm and squeezed it gently. He was feeling something so, *so* deeply. "Don't be frightened," she whispered. He must have been feeling the love and absence of his grandfather, and Monsieur Pufont was a wonderful man.

Luc stared at the strap, a confused look on his face, and Piaf knew what he was thinking: *Why?* Why did the smell from the doctor's oily hand bring a good memory back to the boy, and not a horrific one of ghosts and smothering? There was a noise, clinking glass, louder this time.

"Hide!" cried Piaf. "Now!" She spun in a circle.

"Good afternoon, young man! On your feet!" The doctor's voice floated up the tunnel towards them. His words, though hollow from the distance, were coated in a sickly fake sweetness, just like the first time she'd heard him speak at her roaster. "We have a busy night ahead of us!"

"The chatière! The chatière!" blubbered the boy through a mouthful of falling tears.

Piaf's searching eye raced around the room. "What's a chatière? Where?"

The boy quickly nudged her out of his way and slid to one side a wooden tray that hung from a nail high up on the wall. He used his sleeve to wipe tears from his face. "It's a shortcut, like a cat-flap. Secret passages that link tunnels everywhere – carved out by people long dead – there are over one hundred in the sixth arrondissement alone."

Hidden behind the wooden tray was the entrance to a rectangular shaft. Cut out of hard rock, it was not much wider than their bodies, and a cold, dusty air breathed out of it, stinging Piaf's eyes.

The Button Maker scrambled across the room, grabbing a miniature oil-lamp and a small hessian sack. "Tie your bag to your ankle – like this – and get in, quick!" He wrapped the rope of his sack around his ankle. "I'll follow," he said.

Luc tied Piaf's bag roughly to her ankle. "Get in!" he squealed. He bent down and clasped his hands together, waiting for Piaf's foot to heave her up. Her eyes were wild yet firmly focused on the main tunnel with its museum of objects through which they had arrived. Footsteps! The doctor was too near.

First Piaf, then Luc, shimmied into the tiny chatière shaft. The space was so tight, Piaf could not turn nor twist. Nor fidget. Her arms were pressed tight against her sides, and she had to point her toes to stop her heels scraping the roof. She squirmed forward like a worm, praying she was leaving enough room for the boys behind her. Then what little light had entered the shaft disappeared.

She heard muffled words, and held her breath.

The boy was still out there. She heard him sniffle, loudly, before he spoke.

"Bonjour, Doctor," he said. "Let me help you with that." There was a clinking sound, like Monsieur Auguste's wine glasses, only more delicate.

"Careful," said Dr Le Chandelier. Silence followed. Then the doctor spoke in such a kind way, Piaf could picture him placing his long fingers on the boy's shoulder or ruffling his hair, just as he had done to her in Hôtel-Dieu. "Have you been crying, my boy?"

His "boy" muttered something she could not hear.

"Good lad. I bring no food, but will reward you later – we have more urgent business to attend to, I'm afraid. It seems we need to repeat our experiment and increase the dosage. The air in the Overground is not quite repaired." The sound of glass clinking smashed its way past Piaf and slid down the pitch-black shaft before her. "As before, you need to set up one bottle beneath each entonnoir."

"*Air-hole*," explained Luc from behind, his voice little more than a wispy breeze. Piaf's memory tinkled with the sound of broken glass she had scooped away from the air-hole they had found.

There was another tinkling sound, this time not in her head. It was the sound of the doctor's fingernails tapping glass, just as the nurse had done to Papa's syringe on that awful day. "This here is a new dosage," said the doctor. "Careful now, these bottles are delicate. Stand back when you remove the cork or you will interrupt the flow. Set them up now beneath each entonnoir and, at nightfall, my boy, fog the city."

Piaf gasped – *fog!*

She felt Luc tug on her money bag – he'd heard it too. Just like how Madame pulled a thread to tighten ruffles in fancy cuffs and collars, Piaf could feel the links between countless memory boxes contract until they collided with each other: yesterday morning's fog – how it didn't entirely melt away despite the sharp October sun, covering all of Paris in a stubborn buttery layer; how it squirmed like thick vanilla cream in the potholes where Rue du Dragon met Boulevard Saint-Germain; how the Oxygène in Dr Le Chandelier's canister back at the asylum had done the very same thing, and how it had robbed her brother of his memory; Maman's memory loss, Madame and Monsieur Pufont's too; the Miracles Parisiens and the white Notre-Dame and the year that everyone forgot.

The fog and the doctor's Oxygène were made of the same thing.

"The doctor poisoned *everyone*." Piaf whispered so quietly it tickled her gritted teeth. "He did it. He did it. He—"

"WHERE DID YOU GET THIS?" The change in the doctor's tone sent a chill through Piaf's bones.

"Erm, the candle?" said the boy.

Piaf balled her fists and pressed her forehead into the dirt. She wanted to kick herself. The simple candle with its simple Sainte-Chapelle crest had nearly gotten them caught in the Grande Châsse by *not* being there. Now, thanks to her, it was centre-stage.

"I… I think I can't remember, Doctor…" offered

the boy, his voice quivering. There was a small scraping sound as the boy backed up to the chatière's wooden tray, slowly shifting it to one side. A tiny crack of light entered the shaft.

The doctor grunted. "Why do you have a sack tied around your ankle? People only tie their wares around their ankle if they are using a chatière. Are you going somewhere?" Piaf heard the doctor kick something.

"I ran out of root-wood, so I was going to search for more," said the boy. Piaf cringed; even she knew the room was packed with large chunks yet to be carved.

The doctor cursed, the words rotten. "Is there a chatière in here?" Piaf heard wooden cups and plates clunking as they were tossed to the ground. Her heart pounded against the cold stone. The doctor trashed the room as he searched for a tunnel so small that a boy had the need to tie his bag to his foot.

"WHERE ARE THEY?"

There was a *smack* out there, like something hard had been thrown at flesh. Every muscle in Piaf's body tensed. She wanted to back out – back out of the tunnel and save the poor boy. Oh, what had she done?

Light suddenly poured into the shaft, finding its way past Luc and turning Piaf's view from black to chocolate brown. "MOVE!" cried the boy as he squeezed himself into the chatière.

Luc slapped Piaf's bare feet. "GO, PIAF! MAKE ROOM!"

Piaf used her hands by her sides to heave herself forwards, the enormous effort gaining her only inches. She kept going and going, listening to the cries of their new friend as the doctor's arm reached in and clawed at his legs and then his hessian sack, no doubt ripping the skin from his ankle.

"GRAB MY LEG!" cried Luc to the boy, and he too grabbed Piaf's. As the doctor tried with all his might but failed to fit inside the small chatière tunnel, three against one finally worked and the doctor broke his hold.

They squeezed forward, on and on, like blind worms through the jagged rock, arms pressed by their sides and heads turned to one side. Piaf spat. Sticky cobweb silk and something chalky caked her mouth as she dragged herself up through the seemingly never-ending shaft.

They were climbing, steadily.

When they reached a flatter section, the boy eventually flicked on his oil-lamp and spoke.

"My name is Bertrand Pufont, and I am the Button Maker from Pufont's Button Bijouterie. But yes, Mademoiselle Chestnut Roaster, you can call me Bertie."

Twenty-five | Vingt-cinq

The Chatière, Beneath Rue Vavin, Montparnasse, Paris

Piaf stopped heaving her way through the tight shaft. Only for there not being room for her tummy to do so, she wanted to laugh out loud at Bertie's words; he had called her *Mademoiselle Chestnut Roaster* – a name far too big for her. "You can call me Piaf!" she panted.

"And I'm Luc."

"Bonjour Piaf, bonjour Luc," said Bertie from behind. "I am pleased to meet you." Though his words were polite, they were dampened by a confusion Piaf struggled to comprehend. What would it be like to suddenly remember a life you never knew you had? Poor boy must be in shock. She heard him sniffle and groan.

"Bertie?" The smack she'd heard before Bertie entered the shaft was slapping around her mind, waking up memories of a wicked schoolteacher she'd once endured. "Did he hit you?"

"No," said Bertie. "I hit him," and Piaf knew by his voice he was smiling, so she smiled too as she heaved on and on through the chatière until her fingers throbbed too much and her knees stung the smile away. Unable to fidget, memories of that same schoolteacher trapping her fluttering hands beneath the lid of her hinged desk, and trapping her feet beneath its two front legs, rattled across her mind. To stop it, she counted every heave forward and was surprised when, somewhere further back in the chatière shaft, she heard Luc and Bertie count too.

When they'd counted to one hundred, she had to ask, "Are we there yet, Bertie?" A *short-cut* he had called it, and she could not help but huff out loud.

"Nearly," grunted Bertie from close behind Luc. "But, from here on, don't shout, s'il vous plaît, and don't touch the ceiling. It's fragile."

"Fragile?" Piaf mouthed. How could hard, jagged rock, that left the skin of her back, knees and elbows red-raw while it boxed her in like a coffin, be *fragile*? It was a word she'd been called time and again: by doctors because she'd failed to grow since the last visit; by teachers who'd said her "little brain" would struggle to keep up with "normal" kids her age; and of course, Maman, fearing she'd be trampled in a crowd – *mind your sister, Luc, she's fragile*, she'd say, even blessing herself like Madame Legrand. With every wiggle forward, the fragile rock closed in, tighter and tighter. She placed her hands flat beneath her shoulders and slid herself onward, but then she froze.

"What was that?"

"Shh, s'il vous plaît!"

There was another jolt. She felt it in her stomach – like the ground had hiccupped. She pressed her cheek down on the cold dirt: a buzzing, a vibration. While she fought off the memory of yesterday's game of hide and seek inside the Grande Châsse and the vibrations of Sainte-Chapelle's grouchy knight, the rock hissed and cracked and began to tremble.

"Luc? Bertie?"

Was this it? Was this how it would end, trapped

goodness knows how many metres underground? Fear gripped her breath. Bertie whispered something she could not make out.

"What, Bertie? What? Are we about to die?" Memories lined up like a monstrous deck of cards, ready to flick every single one before her – her entire *life*. "GO AWAY!" she yelled at her memories, wishing she had her squirrel button to twist.

"SHUSH!" It was Luc. "It's all right, Piaf. Bertie says this happens every few minutes in this part of the shaft, and plenty of other parts, too," he whispered, passing on the young Button Maker's underground expertise. The tremble grew into a shake and Luc's voice rose as he spoke. "Something to do with the broken overground air, he thinks."

Piaf imagined the falling stars, pounding down towards them from above, splitting the air into broken shards, smashing through stone to get to them – like a great big, speeding monster... "On tracks!" Piaf finished her imaginings out loud. She puffed out a breath of relief – what had she been thinking? There was no broken air! No monster! And no Great Leonid Meteor Storm!

"It's only a steam engine! We're under the railroad!

Wait till Maman hears about this!" she said, picturing Maman holding her own heart. "*You'll be the death of me*, she'll say!" Of course, she'd imitated Maman of old, not new Maman, a memory reminded her, and her heart sank. Maman was helping a man who had not only snatched twenty children, he had poisoned all of Paris. A man who had robbed everyone of a precious year of memories. And, if she heard him correctly, he was planning to do it all again – this time with a "stronger dose". *Fog the city*, he had said to Bertie, and his words were stamped across every tunnel and alleyway in her mind.

Piaf found herself scratching harder at the shaft's dusty surface. She squirmed faster, and faster. She needed to prove to Maman and the world what the doctor was doing, and now that they had Bertie, they could do that, couldn't they? She wanted out – out of this shaft and out of Paris's underground twin. Soon as they were able, she would look at the map and search for a great big exit sign, wherever that might be. But then her memory displayed the sad face of the girl with the crooked nose as though she were there, inches from her face. Her heavy lids, her pale, pale skin. The chain.

There was no way Piaf could go home without her.

The air that washed down the shaft towards her grew colder and, as it swished past her hot face, she swore it carried the words *hurry, this way* with it. It urged her to keep going. Smaller than the boys, she quickly gained some distance, clawing her way towards it. Without the benefit of light, it came as a shock when she realised her head was dangling over absolutely nothing. She squeezed her hand up by her side and held it out in front. Pins and needles coursed through her arm as she swung it wildly up and down and all around. Space.

Something solid above her head – a pole perhaps – was jutting out of the wall outside the shaft. She grabbed it and inched herself out.

Luc soon reached her, his shape a shadow in Bertie's light. "What in hell are you doing, Piaf?"

Piaf was dangling from the pole, her face staring back down into the rectangular chatière shaft. Her body felt free and she let it kick and sway and shake all it wanted.

Bertie's light caught her eye. "Careful, Piaf! There's a bit of a drop down, so grab your knees if yo—"

"PIAF!" roared Luc.

Piaf disappeared down into the darkness.

She landed awkwardly on something, but that something didn't hurt – whatever it was, it clunked and cracked like fine shards of pottery beneath her. The surface began to crumble away with her weight, the same way a fresh macaron at Ladurée's on Rue Royale would do when she couldn't resist finger-poking it.

It took her several seconds to detangle her flapping arms, her legs already a lost cause. "HELP!"

"Try not to move!" cried Bertie from inside the shaft.

"She can't *not* move!" said Luc. He felt for the pole in the darkness and swung himself out. "I'M COMING!"

"Wait!" Bertie scrambled after him to the edge of the shaft and shone his light out.

Dangling, Luc screamed, "AGH! NO!" It was a horrid cry, just like the one he'd done when he remembered his snippet of lost memory. Maybe he'd seen another ghost? Piaf watched as he grappled for the shaft, forcing Bertie and their only source of light back into it. Rather than come save her, Piaf could see her brother's desperation to go back the way they came. Why on earth would anyone want to go back?

"Luc! Bertie!" cried Piaf, "I'M DOWN HERE!" Her eyes followed the arc of Bertie's light as it searched her out, scanning down the wall, highlighting every block until it reached her, and what she saw – along with a dreadful retch – quickly silenced her.

Bones.

Millions of them.

Twenty-six | Vingt-six

The Bone Well,
Beneath Montparnasse Cemetery, Paris

They were in her armpits. They were wrapped around her neck and they stabbed at her ribs. Finger-bones dug into her hair; skulls with empty, cracked eye sockets stared her down. Piaf had landed in a massive jumble of skeletons.

She yelled, her arms swinging out wildly. A memory box labelled *sinkhole* charged to the front of her mind, waving an image of her hastily-made torch of bone and cuff so closely she was sure she could smell singed hair.

"Don't worry!" cried Bertie. He pulled himself

out of the chatière shaft and clung to the wall like a spider – ten months underground had taught him well. He reached down to a skull protruding from the wall itself and patted it like a pet. "Dead people can't hurt you…" His feet, one with the hessian sack still in tow, knew precisely where to go as he climbed down, finding footholds in the dim light. "Unless it's the ghost of Philibert Aspairt, of course – he got lost down here nearly one hundred years ago according to a stone I once found. His story was carved into it, and I reckon he wrote it himself. Very neat writing."

"THAT'S NOT HELPING!" yelled Piaf.

"And I'd swear he spies on me sometimes," Bertie added. He froze for a moment. "I can *feel* him, staring at me from the darkness." And Piaf came to think of the floating light that had appeared and beckoned her on just after Luc had told her she was a star that had floated down to his side. Bertie balanced himself on the uneven surface of bones, reached for Piaf's hand and pulled her out with ease. It made a racket that echoed away like falling dominoes.

"We're in hell," cried Luc, as he made efforts to climb down, retracing Bertie's exact footsteps. "We've gone too deep. This is hell, isn't it?" He pulled so hard at his tight shirt Piaf heard it rip.

"No, not hell," said Bertie. Piaf struggled to balance as Bertie tentatively released his grip on her to help Luc. She briefly likened herself and Luc to the helpless, lost tourists who would often congregate on her corner at Rue du Dragon, adding chaos to their roaster's queue. "We're in the Bone Well," said Bertie, "at the very edge of my arrondissement." He held his lamp skyward, and swirled it, highlighting the circular shaft of a huge well. "See?"

Piaf and Luc stared up. Rather than an idyllic full moon and perhaps a steel bucket on a rope, a big glut of suspended mud and bones entirely blocked the exit of the well. As though it were disturbed by their presence, one skeleton's ribcage crashed down before them.

Piaf was sure her heart slipped sideways. "What *is* this place?"

"There's a cemetery up there – *Montparnasse*," explained Bertie. "They buried too many bodies in it, you see, so they're sinking down into every gap they can find. I think. At least the rats have eaten most of the rotten bits."

205

Piaf retched again, loudly. Chalky bone dust had lined her throat like fur. She shook from head to toe as she turned on the spot, taking in her creepy surroundings. She backed into Bertie, bones crunching and rolling underfoot.

"Pardon," she said, abruptly. "How do we get out of here?"

"It's all right. We're safe here – Doctor can't follow. He's too big for the chatière and it will take him longer to arrive through the tunnels."

"How do we get out of here?" repeated Piaf. "We really need to keep moving – we have a girl to find and a city to save! Didn't he say he was going to fog it again? And… and— oh, where is the way out?" She threw a sideways glance at the boys to see if they'd noticed the shake in her voice. She really did not want this place to be part of their "adventure" and knew well that a memory box had already polished itself inside and out, ready for juicy, bony content to play for her over and over again.

Bertie stared at her. She wasn't sure if it was pity or something else in his eye.

"Just because I am small, it doesn't mean I am scared," she huffed. Her finger was pointing straight at him. She knew he could see its tremble, and that made her blood boil. She quickly ducked down to untie her money bag from her ankle.

Bertie nodded. "Ants are fearless too." He'd said it in the same way Luc would rattle off facts, and his words took Piaf by surprise. Did he *really* think she was fearless?

Bertie pointed behind her towards a small, jagged hole in the wall of the well. It was so black, Piaf wondered if it was there at all. "There's a way out through there…" said Bertie. This time it was his finger and his words that trembled, "… but I've never crossed into another arrondissement because that is the rule. Doctor begged me not to risk leaving the sixth – it's *perilous*, Doctor told me, and he didn't want me to get hurt. Besides, he needs my help to fix the Overground." He cupped his hand across his forehead and cried something – it seemed the underground world that he'd known for the guts of a year was raging war with his new-found memories of his life with Monsieur Pufont.

"Your justification is flawed," said Luc in much the same way those court men in wigs spoke at their roaster. And Luc didn't drop it there, force-feeding

Bertie with the facts of what had and hadn't happened, so Piaf silenced him with a thump that made Bertie shriek. "*What*, Piaf?" snapped Luc, "People need to know when they have their facts wrong."

It struck Piaf there and then that Luc could no more hold back stating facts and correcting people than she could stop picking, flicking, tapping, counting or whatever the moment called for. "I'm sorry."

Still staring at the black hole, Bertie slapped his own cheeks. "And what if there is broken air in there? Or no air! Or—"

"*Or* what if the girl with the crooked nose is through there?" said Piaf. "We *must* find her, Bertie – between her story and yours, we'll have all the proof we need to convince everyone of what Dr Le Chandelier has done. We can't leave the girl behind – especially not now because the doctor knows we are on to him."

"She's talking about the girl the doctor stole," explained Luc, on seeing Bertie reach for his own nose. "She gave Piaf the leaf skeleton—"

"OH NO!" cried Piaf. She wiggled all her fingers in the light of Bertie's lamp. "It's gone!" Her fingers suddenly felt icy cold and bare, stripped of the leaf skeleton and its warm yet weightless hug. She searched through her bag, sending loose coins tinkling down through the bones into the depths of the well, casting off a wish while she was at it. Where was it? She'd felt lost enough *with* it, never mind without. She found both sides of the wooden burr and held them up. "Empty!"

Bertie's little finger appeared before her eyes, "Is this what you are looking for?" The leaf was wrapped around his finger and a memory blossomed in Piaf's mind: how she used to cling onto Maman's little finger as they walked through busy streets, squeezing it twice for *je t'aime* each time they stopped at a junction. Would Maman still do that?

A little tear blurred Piaf's eye as she gently unwrapped the leaf. As though the leaf, too, was afraid of its surroundings, it quickly wound itself around her finger and clung on tight. "We need to look at the map again. Find our bearings," said Piaf. A scattering of bone dust rained down. "But not here."

"Wait, s'il vous plaît!" Bertie rummaged in his sack and pulled out another small oil-lamp. He plucked away shards of broken glass before handing it to Piaf. "I'm not sure how long it will last. I was returning it to Doctor for repair."

Piaf lit the lamp and clenched its curved handle tight. Before its flame had even stretched, there was a loud *clop*, not unlike that of the hollow burr as it hit the floor of the Grande Châsse, and not unlike Madame's Russian dolls; it sounded like bone on bone, and it came from the other side of the black hole.

"What was that?" said Luc.

Bertie gulped. "The ghost of Philibert Aspairt?"

Twenty-seven | Vingt-sept

Empire of the Dead,
Beneath Montparnasse Cemetery, Paris

"I'm going in," said Piaf. She rubbed her arm where Maman's worried grip would normally hold her back. Feeling a mix of adrenaline and pride, she suddenly remembered the day Papa had let her ride a two-wheeler in the Jardin du Luxembourg for the first time. *Freedom.* She squeezed through the gap in the Bone Well's wall with ease. Inside, the tunnel was her height and would offer enough room for the boys to crouch as they walked. She held her stuttering lamp out before her.

"Are you in here, girl with the crooked nose?"

Only a few steps inside, the tunnel grew in height. Soon, a wide stone plinth hung from the roof like a welcome sign. "*Arrêtez*," Piaf read, and that is what she did – she stopped. The letters were etched out and serious, like words on a headstone. She read the next bit. "*This is the Empire of the Dead.*"

She gulped and entered a round room.

Piaf's jaw hung open. The walls were lined with thousands of human bones but, unlike the Bone Well, the bones here were clean, the colour of teeth, and arranged in an impressive pattern: skull – the end of a leg bone – then a smaller bone – the end of another leg bone – skull. The row above it was arranged in the same order, only one step across to the right. Maman's knitted winter shawls had a similar pattern, a box reminded her.

"You need to see this!"

The ground was smooth, as though it had been brushed. She darted around the room, one full circle. Three tunnels intersected the walls and, between each, were fascinating bone displays built into the walls themselves: one, a large cross, etched with dates hundreds of years old, then a heart shape made of skulls, and finally a huge wheel, its spokes made of long, thin bones. In the centre of the room stood a column, as wide as it was tall, that appeared to support the ceiling. It too was entirely clad in bone. Piaf felt dizzy as she found herself counting its skulls as they wrapped around it in a mesmerising swirling pattern.

At the column's foot, sitting on the otherwise clean ground, were the bones of a hand. It looked out of place, as if it had just fallen from someone's pocket, with a loud *clop*. Just like the sound they had heard from the Bone Well.

Piaf quickly held her lamp high – was someone else here?

"Tell me what is going on, s'il vous plaît."

Piaf swung around to find Bertie sitting on a majestic throne, also made of bones.

"Oh my!" she said, studying the throne. It was beautiful, only for the remains of dead people. Bertie placed his lamp on the ground so as not to blind her and she did the same until they were looking at each other, eye to eye.

Bertie rubbed his temples. "So, I know I have Grandpère." Piaf saw his eyes flick towards her bag's strap. "And I'm Bertie, the Button Maker." The poor boy looked so confused. "When I carve, there's an ugly stage that has to happen before it starts to take shape. It's like my memories are stuck there – half-formed, unfinished, *incomplète*. There are too many gaps to make sense of it. It all feels like a dream I once had."

"It's not a dream." Luc said it so surely that not even Bertie could question it.

Bertie seemed to not notice Piaf's jittering limbs and twiddling fingers as she explained everything to him – how he was stolen nearly a year ago, how his grandfather would have mourned his loss, and how, ten months later, a great fog stole the memories of all Parisians so that his grandfather woke up to the horror of Bertie's loss once again. All by the hand of a cruel doctor. She didn't bother to tell him about how the doctor now hunted her, how he had plans to create something for the Exposition Universelle this spring. None of that would help Bertie now, so she kept it all about him. There was a long silence when she had finished, only broken by her stomach's loud rumbles.

Piaf glanced at one of the tunnels. They really

needed to get going – the doctor had plans and she wasn't planning on letting him get away with it anymore. They needed the girl.

"Wait," said Bertie. *"A hungry horse stalls its cart,* Grandpère told me that. We'll find your girl faster if we eat."

Piaf smiled – Madame had said the very same to her countless times when she'd ask Piaf to sample bite-sized prunes soaked in some new spice she'd found. Madame and Monsieur Pufont were dear, dear friends and she now wondered who'd told who those words first.

Bertie quickly opened his sack and shared with them small packages wrapped in paper and string. Inside hers was a corner of dry bread. It smelled of nutmeg and cinnamon, and, reluctantly, she forced herself to twist her button to rid her mind of the joys of Madame Legrand and her spice-filled Moroccan dishes.

After a few seconds of eating and thinking, Bertie stopped chewing. "I don't understand," he said. *"Why?* Why would Doctor take me? Why would he poison everyone like you say? He takes good care of me – medicine, clothes, food." He held up his bread.

"*Good care?* Dr Le Chandelier?" said Luc. He pointed to Bertie's ankle – his sock was shredded and burn marks circled his skin where the doctor had tugged his hessian sack as they made their escape.

"He stole you because you are gifted," said Piaf. "You are your grandfather's apprentice after all, and your grandfather is the owner of *the* Pufont's Button Bijouterie. I'm sure you must be the best button maker in Paris. People just don't know it yet. The doctor took other gifted children too. Twenty in all."

Bertie sat up straight and sighed. "Doctor told me he was trying to help me – that I'd lost my memory when the air broke and he'd be able to fix it. I can remember being down here for months, but as for my life up there? All I have are the few memories I got when you made me smell that." He pointed to the strap of Piaf's bag.

Piaf pulled the strap over her head and handed it to Bertie. "You need to try smelling it again. Just there." She pointed to the four oily finger marks on its surface. "Whatever that oil is, it came from the doctor's hand."

Luc shuffled where he stood, and Piaf did not miss it.

She watched as Bertie breathed in the smell deeply, just as people would do as they passed her roaster. Suddenly her own head filled with the strong scent of roasting chestnuts, mingling with wafts of strong coffee from Les Deux Magots and singed cloth from Pufont's Button Bijouterie. It all made her inhale so deeply she feared her lungs would burst.

The throne crackled as Bertie slouched back into it. "More memories," he said. "My Grandpère. He sings while he works. He eats frogs legs every Tuesday. He wears a silver brace of diamante on his ankle when he cycles." Memories widened his smile. "Grandpère told me you adore my buttons – you were my first customer, though we'd never met, so I carved more… just for you. I hate nougat…"

Then Piaf spotted the precise moment Bertie recalled the reason why they had never met before – the reason why he had chosen to hide himself away in a small, cluttered room above the button shop: the death of his parents. Piaf knew what he needed, and she didn't care that they had only just met. She reached in and hugged him tight. Soon Luc wrapped his long arms around them both and a thought struck Piaf: did Luc know of Papa's passing? As she told him, neither Luc nor Bertie moved, and the threesome stayed that way, like a tight ball of wintering squirrels.

Twenty-eight | Vingt-huit

For the first time, ever, Piaf felt the unbreakable connection she always had with Luc extend out like tiny, grasping vine shoots to someone else their own age – to Bertie. Not once had Bertie sneered at her constant fidgeting, her shuffling and her counting. Not once had he mocked or ignored her for being so small. In fact, he made her feel worthy and brave. And now, they had something profound in common – the great loss of dear family. She knew Luc felt the connection happen too, especially now that she had told her brother, ever so gently, of the loss of their own Papa. Though they had suffered loss, wasn't this the beginning of something new? A *friendship*.

Bertie smiled and looked at Piaf's strap. "*That* is a cure to whatever Doctor did to me. The more I smell it, the more I remember…"

Without saying anything, Luc took the money bag from Bertie's hands. He turned his back to them. Within seconds he'd dropped it to the ground and was ploughing his hands up and down his forehead to shake thoughts away. Piaf knew that, once again, his one hazy memory of the girl ghost and the smothering had paid him a visit.

Luc hung his head low. "Why does it work like a cure for you, Bertie, but not me?" He sounded so sad, Piaf could feel the weight of it in her bones.

The silence was loud.

"Let's find the girl and get out of here," Luc finally said. "Which way do we go?"

Piaf quickly unfurled the leaf skeleton and handed it to Bertie. "Hold it over your lamp."

The high domed ceiling came alive with twisting tunnels and hidden chambers but it was even larger and more defined this time, for it was in the steady hands of a boy who could carve to perfection a hook-and-eye on a minuscule shoe.

"Sensationnel!" cried Bertie.

Piaf stood up and began to follow the lines. "The tree," she said, pointing up to the symbol that led them to Bertie's nest. "That's you, Bertie. Whoever made this map knows that you live there, carving wood. I think the girl might have been right *there*..." She pointed to the tiny dot not far from the tree, the spot where they'd found an airhole and heard Luc's poem. "We saw a light moving near it but, when we followed it, we found you instead."

"That dot is an entonnoir..." said Bertie, "...where I release Doctor's special fog. He calls it his—"

"*Oxygène*," said Luc.

"Yes. It comes in small bottles, and it fixes broken air. Or so I thought, mon Dieu." He sighed at his shame and then pointed to the dot. "That is the longest entonnoir, and it goes all the way up to the Overground, nearly twenty metres up. The other entonnoirs are shorter—"

"*Other?*" asked Piaf. As soon as Bertie had said it, her eye was drawn to more dots that spread out like a halo around the symbol of the tree. She saw a glut of dots some distance to one side of it. "Where's that?"

"Street names are carved into some rocks down here so you know what's above, and that is the junction of Rue du Dragon and Boulevard Saint-Germain," said Bertie. Piaf caught Luc's eye – Bertie was speaking of *their* corner: Rue du Dragon.

She noticed Bertie's cheeks suddenly redden.

"I drilled too many holes there," Bertie continued. "I reckoned the more I made, the better, but Doctor got cross. I just wanted to make sure the Oxygène's fog would get everywhere so he would be pleased, but he told me I was weakening found nations or something."

"*Foundations*," corrected Luc. "It's what holds up buildings. Bad foundations would make a building collapse."

The box labelled *sinkhole* dominated Piaf's mind once again, and she knew precisely why – Bertie's entonnoirs were to blame for what had happened on her corner at Rue du Dragon – but she reached down and twirled a piece of chipped bone to keep her attention with the boys. "Your Oxygène fog got everywhere, Bertie; biggest fog I ever saw," she said, feeling the need to reassure. "You did a good job."

"A good job of robbing everyone in Paris of a year's worth of memories," said Luc. "Sorry," he added on seeing another wave of shame wash over their new friend.

"I can't believe I did that to everyone."

Piaf put her hand on Bertie's shoulder. "And the doctor is planning on doing it again. Isn't that what he said to you, Bertie?"

"At nightfall. There is no way he could do it alone. Could he?" Bertie looked at Piaf, as if she'd know the answer. "It's far too much for one person! He'd need help to place all the bottles under all the entonnoirs – guess how many there are in the sixth arrondissement! He'd need my help."

"Maybe not *your* help," said Luc. "Look at that dot." He pointed to something on the map's shadow close to where he stood.

"That's not in the sixth arrondissement," said Bertie with a frown. "I didn't drill that one. I'm not allowed go outside the sixth." He scratched his head.

"Precisely." Piaf gasped. "Look!" She ran to the other side of the room. "There! And there!" She pointed towards countless more dots evenly spaced

223

throughout the entire map. If she squinted and erased everything but the dots from her vision, their pattern reminded her of the black dots in the lace on Maman's funeral hat.

In the centre of each halo of dots was a tiny symbol.

"You're not the only one down here."

Bertie nodded, "You mean the girl with the crooked no—"

"Not just her. That tree symbol is you, right?" Piaf dashed around the room, jumping and pointing every time another symbol came into focus. "There! Is it a cat, or a dog? That's someone else, Bertie!" she cried. "And there! That's a musical note! And there!"

"I think there's an abacus over here!" added Luc, his head thrown back as far as it would go. "And are they ballet shoes?"

"Twenty symbols, twenty arrondissements," said Bertie.

Heat drained from Piaf's skin. "*Twenty* children went missing."

Exasperated, the rattling boxes in her mind that flapped newspapers, with their shocking headlines of missing children over the past year, settled down and closed their lids with a ferocious bang.

Piaf's eyes jumped from symbol to symbol.

"And we've just found them."

Twenty-nine | Vingt-neuf

Within seconds, Piaf was linking the map's symbols to stories hoarded deep in her memory – things Maman had told her while she'd combed her matted hair, newspaper articles she'd read while rolling cones for her chestnuts, and gossip she'd overheard at her roaster. Stories of *missing children*.

"Maman told me about a boy who had the voice of an angel. He went missing when he went carol singing last Noël down by the Place de la Concorde." She pointed to the musical symbol on the floating map overhead. "Do you think that could be him? And the Paris Opera scandal – that was on the cover of *Le Petit Parisien* for three solid days – their youngest dancer disappeared."

Luc said nothing but pointed up to the tiny, etched-out ballet shoes.

Piaf marched over to the other side of the map. "There was a ten-year-old girl who could do the sums of a grown-up, and she went missing last March." Piaf found her voice rolling faster and faster – these weren't just symbols: they were real people with real lives. She stared up at the symbol of the abacus. "*That* could be her. Monsieur Auguste said she'd run away, that she didn't want to take part in the Enfants Surdoués Showcase at the Exposition Universelle this spring." Piaf instinctively ducked when the shadow map violently flickered.

She turned to look at Bertie – perhaps he'd hiccupped as he held the leaf.

"*Enfants Surdoués Showcase?*" said Bertie, echoing Piaf's words. His eyes were wide.

"That's where gifted children are exhibited on stage at the Expositions," explained Luc.

"They advertised it in the *Le Petit Parisien* newspaper," continued Piaf. "It's disgusting. They're forced to do tricks like the tigers at Parc Zoologique de Paris. People even throw coins." When she looked up again, the map – still in Bertie's hands – was shaking. "Are you all right, Bertie?"

"I had a big argument with Grandpère," he said with a whimper. "It is one of my last memories. He was cross because I wouldn't let him put my buttons in the shop window and he said I'd want to stop hiding in my room because he'd already registered my name with the Exposition Universelle – for the Enfants Surdoués Showcase." His eyes looked like puddles about to overflow. He dipped his head. "I told him he might as well have displayed *me* in his window. Then I threw one of my buttons at it." His shame ran so deep, Piaf could feel it seeping into her own heart. "I also spilled varnish on his new Turkish rug, but that was an accident." He attempted a small smile.

"Monsieur Pufont is very proud of you, Bertie. He told me so, more than once. So proud he just wanted to tell the world." She held up her cuff and imagined her squirrel button dangling down. "You're really gifted," she said. Bertie sniffled and she gave him a minute. While she waited, she looked up at the symbols dancing on the map. "They're all gifted too." She wondered were *they* all registered for the

Enfants Surdoués Showcase? Is that why the doctor stole them? An army of gifted children held captive underground and brainwashed into helping him wipe the city's memories clean with his Oxygène. Something clicked inside.

"We've been doing this all wrong," she said and swore the map swirled overhead, such was the change in her thinking. "We shouldn't be running *from* the doctor – we should be running *to* him. We need to stop him before he gets all these children to release his Oxygène – his forgetting fog – and we need to save every one of them." She stared at the symbols on the map.

"He brought me a big tray of glass bottles – one bottle for each of my entonnoirs. He told me to start releasing them at nightfall. It'll fog everyone's memories away, again."

"This time for more than a year – it's a stronger dose," warned Luc. "Do you think he might have a stronger dose of that oil on his hands – the cure – too?" he hoped. He pulled at his tight collar. "We will need it to help all the children find their memories. The bag's strap might not be strong enough for everyone and they won't want to be saved unless they can remember their past." And Piaf knew he desperately meant himself too.

Bertie looked at Piaf. "What do we do, s'il vous plaît?"

"Start somewhere," said Piaf and Luc together.

Luc pointed to the abacus symbol. "I think we should go there first," he said.

Bertie quickly disagreed, suggesting a symbol of what appeared to be a bridge would be closer, and suddenly they began to bicker like brothers.

"Hold the leaf *still*, Bertie!" cried Piaf. In the very same way that memories fired down alleyways in her mind to awaken other memories, Piaf had found herself tracing the map's tunnels from one stolen child to another. "They all connect up!" she said. "If we ignore all the chatières that the doctor can't use, the tunnels all meet at that point THERE!" She tried jumping, and on her third attempt, Luc's knee was bent, and she was clambering up to his shoulders. She pressed her finger against a tiny, unremarkable junction on the map. There was a round clearing at its centre.

"I don't know where that is," said Bertie, "but I'm sure it would be across the River Seine, in the first arrondissement – probably around the Louvre, or maybe the Jardin des Tuileries."

"That's where we find our chestnuts," said Piaf.

"And that's where you found me," said Luc. "The day I forgot everything."

To shoo that memory away, Piaf spun and spun one of Luc's curls around her finger until he slapped it. "That junction is a *hub*. Like the centre of a wheel. If the doctor is too big to use the chatières, he'll need to go through that hub if he wants to visit any of the children. We don't have time to rescue everyone down here, but if the doctor is planning to fog the city again, he'd have bottles of his Oxygène to deliver across the whole of the Underground. We have to stop him now, before he gets to the children!"

"We are *here*," confirmed Bertie, pointing to another round shape over his bone throne, and Piaf let her eye follow the map's route back to it.

She fluttered down to the ground, threw her bag over her shoulder, and flew at speed down the muddy tunnel between the bony bicycle wheel and the heart of skulls.

Thirty | Trente

The Belly,
Beneath Boulevard des Invalides, Paris

Luc and Bertie did their best to keep up.

Piaf's knees ached as the tunnel dipped deeper and deeper. Another hour later, she swore they were going into the belly of Paris's underground twin, and her feet burned and sweat prickled under her arms despite the air growing damp and chilly. They *had* to catch the doctor. There was no way he would traipse across Paris's overground to get to his stolen children, his arms filled with hundreds of glass bottles. The only way he would go was through the Underground and through that one hub now firmly planted at the forefront of Piaf's mind.

The tunnel split in two.

Strange sounds gurgled towards them from the left one, sending rats scuttering in their direction, and Piaf was relieved the map sent them down the quieter, more respectable one, with its tiny blue mosaic tiles indicating what stood above: *Les Invalides* – one of Paris's grandest mansions. Piaf had never been in it, but Madame had; she'd told Piaf how she'd styled her château's gate posts on the pinnacle at the top of Les Invalides' great dome.

Soon, the smell of the air began to change from earthy and sweet, to the same sour smell Piaf would find on her street corner after rain on a sunny day. Though the ground down here was always cooler than the air, her bare feet now felt too cold and began to slip and slop.

She stopped and held her flickering oil-lamp low. Shallow puddles winked back at her. "Water."

"We must be approaching the river," said Bertie, his words overlapping with their own echo. He was still some distance behind.

Piaf held her light up before her and, for as far as she could see, the light's reflection danced back. There was a rumble and a gushing sound – the same noise that had filled Piaf's head for a whole month after Luc had roared directly into her ear through a metal tube they'd found in the Jardin des Tuileries. Her eardrum had burst, according to Maman, and Luc got into big trouble. Her mind raced from that box to another where Luc had gotten into trouble for correcting the priest who lived three doors down, and then another ...

"PIAF! Did you hear Bertie?" cried Luc. Piaf clenched and unclenched her cold toes to drag herself back to his voice.

"I was asking, what was the weather like up there over the last few days?" Bertie's voice was urgent, impatient.

"It's not really the time to talk about the weather," Piaf called back to him. She looked down – she was unexpectedly ankle-deep in freezing cold water and, unlike the stagnant water elsewhere in the Underground, it was heaving, calmly yet strongly, splashing high as her shins. Like the sea. The noise rapidly grew loud as a lion's roar.

"RUN!" cried Bertie.

Fast as a locomotive, a wave of water chased her down as she ran back up the tunnel towards her brother and Bertie. The tunnel filled with jagged flashes of light as her lamp swung wildly as she ran. The water attacked until, hard as rock, it flattened her, snuffing out the light. She swallowed water so disgusting it heaved back up, taking her breath with it. She swirled and thrashed and yelled. The tunnel filled with her screams and those of countless others as her echo followed suit, until her upper arms were pinched in a vice-like grip and she was hauled out of the water.

"PIAF!" roared Luc. Holding Piaf high, he was balancing on the ridge that ran along the sides of the tunnel. Bertie was panting on the opposite side. Luc bent her over one arm like one of Maman's rugs and smacked her hard between her shoulder blades until a painful cough emptied her lungs of water and she could speak.

"It rained last night," she said, finally answering Bertie's question. The stranger's warning of a storm sprung to mind and she wondered if perhaps he had not made that bit up. "A lot."

Luc began to explain how long it takes for rainwater to travel the length of the Seine before it reaches Paris, but stopped himself when Piaf spluttered. "You are all right," he said, squeezing her tight as a teddy bear. "Remember – we're in this together, and together means we stick together." It was his way of telling her off for running on ahead, but he was finding it way too hard to be cross. She'd seen that before when she'd gotten lost in Le Bon Marché and he'd had to endure Maman's panic until they'd found her in the umbrella shop.

"Hurry, this way," said Bertie, his voice muffled. Piaf climbed down from Luc's warm embrace and balanced, shivering, on the narrow ridge, the water smacking and slapping at her toes. She saw Bertie's bottom half protrude from a chatière, high up on the opposite side of the tunnel. As he disappeared into it, he took the only light with him.

From its entrance, the chatière climbed at a dramatic rate and Piaf's skin burned by the time Luc pulled her out at the other side. Piaf was glad of the warmth as they stood bunched together in a tall, narrow tunnel. They looked left and right. Something was different. At first, she thought it was because they now only had one lamp, but no – the tunnel seemed tinged with blue.

"Entonnoir!" they all said, together.

There was a minor scuffle as they ran towards the source of the dim light.

Piaf won, but dread dropped like a stone inside her. "A glass bottle!" It had been placed directly below the entonnoir. Piaf could see a small drop of oil at its base and a fog, thick as Maman's meringue, swirled above it. The bottle was held in place with two small stones, its tiny cork the only thing stopping the fog from reaching deep into the entonnoir's shaft.

Luc arrived by her side. "Oxygène!"

"This entonnoir belongs to someone else – another missing child," said Bertie. "And the doctor has already given them his orders."

Piaf took the bottle in her hand and used her thumb to ensure the cork was secure before placing it in her money bag. "One down, but how many more to go?" she said. "We need to stop him before he gets to everyone down here, and fast." She stared up into the entonnoir, her urge to keep running suddenly quashed by shockingly cool air powering down the hole. It brought with it taps and clanks from heels far, far above. "People!" she said, somehow shocked to learn that the world was continuing, business as usual.

She sniffed the air hard.

A box in her mind flew open, spraying out perfumes like the fancy ladies with their crystal bottles at Galleries Lafayette. She could smell vine tomatoes and basil, Maman's pillow, oil on Papa's black hands, the palm of her own hand after splitting burrs, and every other favourite smell, even Madame's spice-speckled robe. Yet it was all in her mind. Feeling like her face had been scrubbed clean by Maman's rough face cloth, she stepped back to let Luc and Bertie have their turn.

The tunnel's dusty air quickly smothered her senses like a dirty, wet sponge.

Something tickled her nose. "Can you smell that?" Memory boxes crackled like fireworks – they'd recognised it too. She spun to look at Bertie. Was he eating his bread again? No.

She took the lamp and held it up, lighting up the tunnel further on to their right. It appeared to be a dead end. That smell! She knew they had to find the doctor, and fast, but like being pulled by a rope on a bull's nose-ring, she felt herself walking faster and faster towards the smell. She ignored Luc's repeated calls to stick together, Bertie's warnings to stay close. At the tunnel's end, on all fours, she found a flat shard of rock leaning almost flush against the wall. She let it flop down towards her, sending a cloud of dust into her eyes.

Another chatière.

"I'll be back in a minute," she called back to the boys and carefully wedged the oil-lamp into a hole between rocks. She stuck her head into the chatière shaft – one so small only she would manage – and called with a shake in her voice and a blossoming heart:

"Madame? Madame Legrand?"

Thirty-one | Trente-et-un

Château Legrand,
Beneath the Dôme des Invalides, Paris

A silver teapot with glossy red gems and an elephant trunk handle blocked the exit of the short chatière. Piaf held the teapot in both hands, as Maman always warned her to do, and squirmed out several inches until her head and arms were free.

"An underground room!" she gasped. Deep underground, the square hollow had been excavated out of mud and stone, and, just like the Moroccan spice smell that had hooked her in, everything about it was Madame Legrand.

A single oil-lamp with coloured glass that would put Sainte-Chapelle's windows to shame hung from a plaited rope, its steady flame splashing colour on every surface. All was still and it was silent, like a pharaoh's tomb deep inside one of the mysterious pyramids she'd read about on the back page of the *Le Petit Parisien* newspaper.

Great rugs of terracotta and ochre zigzags carpeted the walls. Sprigs of herbs and dried flowers hung from a fabulous domed roof draped in floaty material. Instantly, Piaf guessed it was the underground twin dome of the most majestic roof in all of Paris: the *Dôme des Invalides*. Like Madame's Russian Dolls, one dome upon a hidden other. And if she was right, all that stood between the two was the buried bones of none other than Napoleon himself. A shiver ran through her like his ghost confirming it true.

A wooden shelf the length of the wall opposite held decorated flowerpots of all sizes – small ones filled with Madame's delicious homemade sweets, two pots either side overflowing with spools of thread, and another with small rolls of rich fabrics, just like the material Madame would bring to Pufont's Button

Bijouterie to match a customer's demands perfectly. The larger pots appeared to be used in lieu of a chest of drawers: stockings in one, each wrapped and bunched like a peony rose; undergarments in the next, and so many scarves heaped high in all the rest – every one she recognised as Madame's. *A place for everything, and everything in its place* – it was Madame's favourite saying and goodness knows how often Piaf had heard it each time Madame paid a visit and tidied the clutter at her chestnut roaster.

Piaf bent at the waist so that she could carefully place the teapot down onto the brightly hand-painted stone floor – each diamond-shaped tile on it different to its neighbour. She saw several were painted with pretty buttons.

She squirmed her way in; the air so thick with spice, it felt hot on her tongue.

There was a table to her left. It appeared to be made of a dark wood, oiled so thickly dead ants clumped at the base of each leg where they'd failed to break free. Terracotta plates with thick glossy rims covered its surface, each holding a perfect cone of spice, some so tall they lined up perfectly with the tip of her nose as she stood before them. The spice cones reminded

Piaf of Madame's great pyramid of colourful spools of threads back in Pufont's – the inspiration behind her own pyramid of chestnuts at her roaster. But Madame's were perfect.

"This is Madame Legrand's home."

There was only one thing missing – her family friend.

"Why didn't you tell me?" Piaf asked the room, wishing Madame there to answer. "You live in a grand château just outside Paris, big as Notre-Dame with rose gardens and a potter's kiln, and your neighbours are Paris's most elite!" she said, imitating her dear friend's proud voice. "That's what you told me!" Clearly, it wasn't true. She wasn't sure how that made her feel. Madame had said she only worked because it was her duty to secure Paris's reputation as the world's most fashionable city. Not for money. "Why would you lie to me? OUCH!" Piaf yelled, having stubbed her toe on one of Madame's Dutch clogs. It was sitting in the middle of the room, on its side. Just the one. Piaf bent down and picked it up. "That's odd," she said, and swung around, searching the room for its match. She stared at the clog, rubbing her finger where Madame's heel had left an imprint on its sole. Madame wore them in place of her velvet slippers since the weather had turned. Boxes rattled, reminding her of every clog Madame had ever worn – like her robe, they were always coated in a dusting of yellow spice that Piaf now realised was not spice at all – it was dust, *underground* dust.

And why would there be only one shoe? "Everything is *not* in its place," she said when she bent down to pick up a small silver medal that had been hidden beneath the clog. She held it and its string of ripped thread between her fingers and pictured ones just like it dangling from Madame's silk headscarf, stuck into the frown lines of her forehead. Worry stabbed Piaf's tummy as she pictured her friend. "Something's wrong, Madame. Isn't it?" she questioned the room again.

She sighed heavily.

Rich spices teased her nose. "ACHOO!" She shook and flapped as the sneeze hit with little warning. "Oh no!" she gasped, soon as her eyes had opened. One of the perfect spice towers was damaged. Did she do that? Its peak was lopsided, and its base avalanched out onto the table. Madame Legrand would be furious. And that's when she saw it – a sparkle protruding from the cone's side. Something was buried deep within the spice.

"I DON'T HAVE TIME FOR THIS!" The doctor's temper-filled roar powered down a tunnel and into the room. Piaf squealed and flapped and rattled and spun in a circle. Where was the door?

A hanging rug with tassels matching the end of Madame's best scarves billowed – it must have been hollow behind it and Piaf sprung back to the chatière like snapped elastic. She swore her toes were still sticking out from it as the doctor ripped the rug from its curtain pole and barged into Madame's home.

"Where did you put it? WHERE? You KNOW that I need it."

Piaf gritted her teeth on hearing his words, each one punctuated by the sound of ceramic crashing on ceramic.

Piaf used her chin, elbows and knees to scoot forwards through the tiny shaft until her head poked out the other side into the blue tinged tunnel.

"Piaf!" cried Luc.

Bertie ran to her and pulled her out.

"It's Madame Legrand!" she cried. "Something is

wrong!" Fear gripped her heart and pounded it against her chest. She knew it must be true, for in her spice-covered hands was something that Madame Legrand would never be without: Empress Josephine.

Thirty-two | Trente-deux

"Are you nearly done?" puffed Luc. Piaf worried for her brother's wobbling legs as he struggled with the weight of Bertie perched on his shoulders. "It's not a button, Bertie! It doesn't need to be perfect!"

"A bit more to the left, s'il vous plaît," said Bertie. He was reaching up to the tunnel's ceiling with Empress Josephine held high. "And Piaf, a little bit steadier with the map, if you can."

Piaf stretched the leaf taut over their one flickering oil-lamp, and held her breath – for once, the shake in her hands was not down to fidgeting. Was Madame in danger? Or worse, was she helping the doctor? Impossible as that might've sounded, the doctor's words were rattling doubt around her head: *You know that I need it*; he'd said it back in Madame's underground home, like they were in it together. Piaf was sure she knew Madame almost as well as her own Maman, from her big soft heart to her sharp points of view, from her giant bear hugs to her colourful life. But then why had she lied about her château?

She swallowed the thought hard: Maman *and* Madame helping the doctor. Tears blurred Piaf's sight, questions grated in her mind, and Bertie scraped and scraped at the coarse rock of the tunnel with the hooked point of Empress Josephine.

One more stroke and Bertie's carving sliced the flickering map's shadow in two with a long waving line etched out beyond it on the tunnel's rock. "Voilà!" he said. "This is the River Seine." He drew an "x" anywhere the shadow's tunnels crossed his etched-out river. "This is the flooded tunnel we tried – it leads directly to the doctor's hub, right there, beneath the Jardin des Tuileries."

Luc rubbed his chin as he scanned the length of the river, "If one tunnel was flooded, they'll all be flooded." He lowered Bertie down, tucked in his shirt and flattened his bunched-up trousers. "But you saw the doctor through there, Piaf," he said, pointing to the chatière only Piaf could squeeze through. "So, he's still able to cross the river somewhere."

Piaf's eye swept along the map's riverside tunnels and, as it did, landmarks overhead sprouted like giants in her mind. "Of course!" she cried. "The Tour Eiffel! The builders spent half of last year beneath it, making sure the ground wouldn't flood – that monster of a thing would sink! It's *huge*," she said. The map's shadow raced around the tunnel as she spoke. She took a moment to reposition the leaf. "Where on the map would the tower be?"

"It was not much taller than the Button Bijouterie last I saw it," said Bertie, sadly. "It's about there," Using the shears he pointed to a cluster of tunnels and entonnoirs further away than Piaf had hoped. To the tower's right was another symbol.

Luc squinted. "I think that's a mouse."

"We'll need to back-track a bit," said Piaf as she packed Empress Josephine into the safety of her money bag, "to the mosaic sign for *Les Invalides* at the beginning of the flooded tunnel, and then take the left tunnel from there." She shivered, having remembered that tunnel with its fleeing rats and strange gurgling sound. *Beware*, she was sure her memory was saying. Could it be flooded too?

"We need to hurry," said Bertie. He apologised for his rumbling stomach. "I'm hungry again and that means it is nearly time for dinner. It is getting late. Nightfall is only a couple of hours away."

No sooner had he said it and Piaf was scooting, sometimes sliding, down the chatière through which they'd arrived. Having left the lamp for the boys to carry, she was riding blind, and, as she neared the end, she recalled that time she ran downhill so fast she couldn't stop. Chatière riding was no different and, howling, she landed in waist-deep river water with a splash.

At the chatière's entrance, Luc's face appeared. She pulled him out and into the cold water. "Sorry, Luc, there's no time for walking on ridges," she said, but she knew he wouldn't mind – not now. The water level soon dropped, and they reached the blue mosaic sign for *Les Invalides*.

Side-by-side, they peered down the adjacent pitch-black tunnel. A rat sat at its mouth as if on watch. It completely ignored them. Bertie held up the lamp, sending his wet sleeve's *drip, drip, drip*, echoing down the winding passageway. Its walls were jagged, like a beast's teeth, and its floor was cracked yet slimy like a pitted tongue.

Fear sprouted horns inside Piaf's chest, and she fiddled and counted hard to beat away anxious memory boxes pounding for attention. Then Luc linked arms with her. Bertie did too. What would she do without them? She steeled herself hard, until the lump in her throat and the horns in her chest melted away.

With every trudged step onwards, the ground rose, higher and higher, until Piaf was sure they were mere strides from reaching the Overground. Piaf's imagination took hold. It blossomed. She imagined the low October sun up there, sinking lower and lower in the sky, playing hide and seek behind the holey legs of the ever-growing Tour Eiffel. She pictured it dipping behind the moon-shaped dome of Les Invalides and casting its orange glow on the chimeras of Notre-Dame. She recalled the strange shadow the sun had cast on the girl with the crooked nose. Sure she could feel the fresh, evening air, she vowed out loud she would find the girl and her snatcher before that sun disappeared.

As if it were summoned, she saw a dim shard of light slicing down through a gap like a metal dagger in the tunnel up ahead. Dust motes and noise poured down with it – engines and shouting and the ever-present deep drone of the city. Her ears had become accustomed to it up there, but here, it rolled like thunder; distant voices clashed like cutlery. Piaf raced to the gap and climbed the jagged wall of the tunnel to reach up to where the light had burst through the highest point of the curved ceiling. The hole was small – too small for Luc and Bertie – but if she let all the air out of her lungs, she would squeeze through.

"Piaf!" called Luc. "Where are you going?"

"Let me see where we are, Luc! We are so close to the Overground! If we are near the river, maybe we can pass over it rather than under." She grabbed at sharp rocks, tugging on them gently first to understand their strength – just as she'd seen Bertie do – and pulled herself up and up through the narrowing gap. Louder and louder the noise came, smells too – the fresh chilly air of Paris had a scent of wet wool and burnt paper with a hint of apple – a smell she had never noticed in her city before.

"I see a metal grate," she shouted back to the boys. Using her fist, she forced the grate up and away.

With her head just below ground level, the brightness of the falling sun stung her eyes. She blinked away tears, as she would do when Maman gave her an onion to chop, and rubbed them hard with her filthy hands until she could see.

Like an ant in its cobblestone-crack nest, she stared up and out at a giant – the four legs of the great and rising Tour Eiffel stood directly overhead, and through its arched legs, the pale grey moon already hung in the blue sky. She twisted her shoulders, unable to squeeze any higher, but from where she clung she could see a whole world. Masses of people had gathered around the tower, waving their hands in prayer. She saw a man faint, another dance; she heard chanting and song. "Miracle!" they cried, "Miracle!" She looked up at the tower. Over the course of the last year – a year everyone had forgotten – it had climbed up and up until it stood like a great big letter A, towering over the buildings of Paris. And to think it was only half way there.

"They think it has grown overnight," said Piaf. Her memory flicked back to one year prior: Bertie was right – the legs were only the height of the Button Bijouterie back then.

Immediately, more boxes rattled, retelling the other "Miracles Parisiens": the white walls of Notre-Dame. Another box leapfrogged to the forefront of her mind – Notre-Dame was once the home of Rapiditus's stolen Cabinet of Oils. Both the Cabinet of Oils and the Tour Eiffel were going to be the centrepieces of the Exposition Universelle next spring.

Piaf instinctively ducked when, like white-tailed eagles on a cliffside, she saw several uniformed knights of the Order of the Holy Sepulchre standing on the highest point of the tower, their white robes flapping in the wind like feathered wings. They were scanning the crowd. Hunting her.

Piaf quietly pulled the grate back in place and lowered herself down.

Thirty-three | Trente-trois

The Oyster Room, Beneath the Tour Eiffel, Champ de Mars, Paris

"It's not safe up there," reported Piaf as she navigated the jagged rocks one step down at a time. "The knights have gathered – lots of them. You hardly think they still believe I stole the Cabinet of Oils?" *Or your brother*, her memory scolded in the doctor's smarmy voice. She climbed lower. "Luc? Bertie?" she cried as soon as her feet had slapped down onto the tunnel floor. Where were they? She spun; a fear-filled memory of that time she was accidentally left alone on a runaway driverless carriage heaved while she waited for her eyes to readjust to the darkness. "LUC?"

Piaf breathed again when she saw the dim light of their one oil-lamp flickering around the bend of the tunnel ahead.

She ran to keep up and smiled when she turned the corner. It opened out to an extraordinarily wide chamber. Gone were the jagged walls of mud and rock – in their place, were buttery lutécien bricks – the very same used at the Place de la Concorde, or *Place de la Révolution*, as Papa insisted on calling it. A guillotine used to sit at its centre, but no such horror faced her now – as she had hoped, the tunnel had been secured against the flooding Seine. Old stone benches lined the walls, and Luc was sitting on one, stretching out his long legs like he was on a swing. She loved how each bench had a smooth dip worn down over hundreds of years – just like the stone steps of Sainte-Chapelle's spiral stairwell, a memory bounced. And just like the kerb she'd heave their roaster up on Rue du Dragon—

"Ouch!" Something had stabbed the heel of her foot. In contrast to the smooth walls and benches, the floor beneath her bare feet was rough and harsh, even to her hardened skin. Bertie held the lamp down low.

"Shells!" cried Piaf. "Oyster shells! Thousands of them!"

"The fishermen on the Seine must have called this home," said Luc. "Looks like they had a feast – for a century or two!" Piaf pictured them perched on their stone benches, just like Luc, slicing open stubborn shells with the points of their sharp knives. Empress Josephine, now tucked away safely in her money bag, would be perfect for the job.

"Why do you not wear shoes?" Bertie asked. Piaf had spotted him staring at her feet several times since they'd met, so she smiled for him when he finally managed to find a polite reason to ask.

"Because they make her feel like a bird in a cage," said Luc before Piaf had a chance to reply, and his words made her heart smile. He didn't know who she was only yesterday, and yet he still *knew* her so well. He stood up beside Piaf, and crossed his wrists before him. He urged Bertie to do the same, and he grabbed Bertie's wrists. Clamped together, they created a cradle.

"A seat, my Queen," said Luc, just as he would say when counting their coins by moonlight in Sainte-Chapelle after a busy day roasting.

Like a throne, they carried Piaf beneath the width of the Seine, well beyond the last of the oyster shells, and onwards until the tunnel walls suddenly changed back to mud and sharp rock. They set her down. They were on the other side of Paris, the side where they would find the doctor's hub somewhere below the Jardin des Tuileries.

Piaf marched on, determined, before the boys. With the oil-lamp in Bertie's hand, she chased her own shadow, and, for a moment, she forgot their plight. She *was* her shadow, a figure stretched big as a giant that wrapped itself around the excavated walls, sliding over ignored rocks that jutted out to graze ankles or bruise shoulders. She leaned forwards and stomped faster and braver. Then something whisked her imagination away and shrank her back to size.

"Can you hear that?" she asked, fearing her mind had taken things a bit too far. A *hush*, quiet but deafening. They all stopped in their tracks.

It grew louder and louder.

Luc spun around. "It's coming from behind us!"

"Non," said Bertie. "It's in front of us!"

Piaf grabbed at her ears and found herself drifting back to the boys. The noise, now swishing and clashing, seemed to emanate from the walls themselves. With the oil-lamp huddled between them, Piaf shrieked when she saw golden lights in the distance, just like the ones she had seen from the sinkhole. Like before, second by second more appeared, and larger and larger they became.

"*Eyes*!" cried Bertie.

"RUN!" roared Luc. He grabbed Piaf's coat and yanked her back towards the way they had come.

"They're behind us!" cried Bertie. All three crashed together in a heap, the lamp snuffed out. In darkness, Piaf found her footing and stood, the floor beneath her the only dependable thing, as something scratched at her feet. Luc? Bertie? It pelted at her shins, climbing higher and higher until whatever it was swirled and wrapped around her body, slapping her face and tangling her hair. *Creatures*. The sound was beastly, like the tunnel itself had emptied its stomach with a guttural roar so deep her screams and those of the boys were drowned out.

She fell forward, like she'd been pushed. Images of the stranger nudging her away from her roaster replayed and replayed in her mind. And now, she felt she was being pushed again. In the darkness, she stumbled forward, then walked and then ran, and when she veered left or right, creatures around her buffeted her back. They nipped at her bare heels, she ran faster, they smacked off her hair, she ran faster screaming at the boys for help. Until, like a cat bored with its injured prey, the creatures stopped dead.

Piaf stood still.

What on earth was going on?

The creatures had brought her here. *Friendly* creatures. A perfect rectangle-shaped line of light stood before her. A door, with light coming from behind. Pyramids of clawing rats slumped to the floor, bats with their golden eyes hung silently from the ceiling where the roots of the Jardin des Tuileries' chestnut trees tangled. Cockroaches and beetles scurried to the sides of the tunnel, clicking until they too silenced. A lone fox circled her legs and snapped at her heels until she edged forward and came to a full stop at the perfectly polished oak door. On it hung a printed sign, clinical in design and identical to the one outside Dr Le Chandelier's asylum office.

"*Apothecary*," whispered Piaf. She nodded her thanks to the creatures. "The doctor's hub."

Thirty-four | Trente-quatre

The Apothecary,
Beneath the Jardin des Tuileries, Paris.

The oak door held on tight before it gave in to Piaf's gentle push. It opened. *Click*. Just a crack, not quite enough to peek inside. Like heat from a roaring coal fire, she was blasted by an explosion of smells: the peel of an orange, a scratched eucalyptus leaf from the Jardin des Tuileries above, Papa's glass of sherry, something harsh and clinical, and rosemary – the smells mixed and swirled together like a bowl of Maman's trifle. Piaf's chest heaved.

The sound of glass smashing from somewhere deep inside crashed into her ears. Her heart pummelled in her chest; memory boxes raged too. Every nerve and every muscle retracted, taking any courage she had with them, and they told her to *shut that door, back away*. She felt Maman's protective strings, reeling her back, too, but when she heard Madame Legrand's voice, something inside her took over.

She glanced behind to tell the boys to only follow when she deemed it safe; she saw Luc, wide-eyed; she saw Bertie, shaking. Next to them, the fox slowly crouched low where it stood, head dipped, legs bent, shoulders hunched as though it were ready to pounce. It briefly dipped its nose, just as Luc would do when telling her to add extra chestnuts to a special customer's order. The fox was telling her what to do. Piaf took heed – she slinked into the doctor's underground apothecary on all fours.

She crawled over the threshold and beyond the point of no return. Stuffy heat enveloped her, and amber candlelight flickered as she stared down at the ground beneath her palms – not mud, but floorboards polished so high they caught her breath in clouds and left smeared prints by the sweat of her hands as she crawled on. The wood did not end there.

She was in a short corridor of sorts; wooden panels flattened the walls and ceiling, erasing all evidence of the Underground. Neat shelves held the traces of muddy boots, and a line of brass hooks lined the walls. A single, black coat hung over her like a floating ghost. And Piaf wondered had she magically arrived in the mud room Madame Legrand spoke of in her château – a mansion whose existence was now clearly in doubt.

"I am *not* going to ask you again," came the doctor's voice. Though it was calm to the point of politeness, it sent shards of shattered glass coursing through Piaf's veins. Something about it was desperate, pleading.

Piaf heard light footsteps padding their way towards her. Should she run? Hide? She jumped to her feet and tried, hopelessly, to disappear into the folds of the doctor's coat. The footsteps stopped and the girl with the crooked nose stood before her.

"The ghost girl!" she heard Luc whisper from beyond the door. "She's the girl I saw in my memory."

Piaf cursed her shaking hands as she urgently unwrapped the leaf from her finger and held it up like an entrance ticket between them.

"It's me, the Chestnut Roaster!" she mouthed, and put a finger to her lips. Her eye was drawn to the small chain dangling from the girl's wrist. Piaf swung her hand behind her back and pointed to the others: *We are here – all of us – and we will save you.*

The girl frowned, deeply. Her icy-blue eyes pierced Piaf like she could see through her. "Oh," the girl said, loud as a lady at Le Bon Marché. "Why is the door open?" She shivered and rubbed heat into her own arms.

Piaf's mouth fell open. *Why?* Why would the girl speak so loudly like that?

The doctor's heavy, fast footsteps clicked like gunshot across the floor. "You started this, Madame Legrand. YOU," he shouted back as he marched on towards the girl with the crooked nose. His muddy boots – in high contrast to his formal black suit – slid as he came to a sudden stop beside her.

Piaf's skin prickled when he smiled at her. "Well, well, well. The Chestnut Roaster," he said. "Welcome – do come in. I am in the middle of something, but you can wait." He walked past Piaf and slammed the door through which she had arrived, the sound of its bolt stabbing the floorboards beneath her feet.

The doctor walked by her again and patted the girl's shoulder. "Well done, Véronique," he whispered into her ear, loud enough for Piaf to hear. "I knew you would bring her to me." He returned to the heart of his apothecary. "Pray tell me, Chestnut Roaster," he called from afar, "what took you?"

Piaf stared at the girl and gritted her teeth. She wanted to scream blue murder at her, but she stalled: Véronique had backed up against the wall and was grasping her hands around her own mouth. Was that regret Piaf could see in her eyes? Or shock? Out of sight, a chair, heavy with someone's weight, honked in desperation across the wooden floor and hooked Piaf's ear.

"Piaf!" It was Madame's voice, but never before had it sounded so small. "Ma plume, ma plume, ma plume."

Piaf must have grown wings. She flew, like a bird of prey, with rage past the girl with the crooked nose, and turned left into the apothecary. It was a large, round space and, like a circle of standing stones around an altar, several oak doors lined the walls. She swished around a spiral of free-standing wooden dressers, each bedecked like trees de Noël with hundreds of tiny glass bottles – tonics, concoctions and tinctures all clinking in her wake. They led her inwards, to the centre of the apothecary, and to the doctor.

At a large round table, Madame sat slumped in a heavy wooden chair. Leather straps bound her wrists to it, and Piaf felt her own chest tighten as though those very straps had slid like a snake and coiled themselves around her. They locked eyes and Piaf gasped – her strong and formidable Madame had been crying. How dare she even think her dear friend had been helping such a beast.

Next to Madame, the doctor flicked at air bubbles in a glass syringe he held, its long needle pointing skyward. He checked his pocket-watch, and a shadow of fear darkened his face and filled his actions with more urgency. "It's quite simple, Madame. If *you* won't tell me where they are, your memory *will*." He slapped the flesh of Madame's arm and aimed his needle. Strapped to the chair, she squirmed and spat and cursed.

"Tell him *what*? Madame! TELL HIM!" Piaf yelled. "Tell him whatever he wants to know!"

Madame shook her head so violently her headscarf unpinned.

Véronique appeared in the corner of Piaf's eye. "Madame, I did not think it would come to this," the girl said. She took a small step towards Madame Legrand. "I'm so sorry I closed it." Her cheeks were red and strands of hair stuck to the tracks of her tears but, however she felt and whatever she had "closed", Piaf could see she did not have the courage to look Madame in the eye.

As the doctor's needle pierced Madame's skin, needle-sharp spikes grated and scratched inside the tunnels of Piaf's mind. *NOW PIAF*, it was screaming like nails on a slate, *the chestnut burr.*

Piaf plunged her hand into her bag and the wooden burr fell into it. She threw it full force at the doctor. It scraped past his forehead and tangled its spikes in his greased-back hair. He grabbed the burr and pulled a clump of hair out with it. He didn't even flinch.

"Last chance to tell me where they are," said the doctor to Madame.

With every cell, Madame refused, and the doctor repositioned the needle.

Piaf gulped. She needed a weapon, a proper one. Her hand dived into her bag again. Every box in her memory slammed shut in protest but she ignored them, and the heavy metal of Empress Josephine kissed her fingers. She held her like a dagger.

"NO, PIAF!" yelled Madame. "Not the Empress!" Her head dipped.

"DROP IT, DOCTOR!" roared Piaf. She pointed the shears at the syringe in the doctor's hand. "DROP IT, NOW!"

The doctor's syringe and its contents smashed to the floor. He lunged towards Piaf, and she instinctively lowered the shears, fearful they would do damage she would regret. He grabbed her by her coat, forced her high in the air and tore Empress Josephine from her grip. A beast-like smile overpowered his face as he dropped her to the ground like a cracked clay pipe.

Crumpled in a heap, Piaf looked up.

He was staring at the shears in his palms, and the realisation that she had handed him precisely what he had been looking for, hit her hard as rock.

Thirty-five | Trente-cinq

Piaf desperately wanted to rush to Madame and tell her how sorry, how foolish, she had been to hand over Empress Josephine so easily. Madame had said the shears were special – but it was only now that she had witnessed the doctor's desire for them, that she realised how special they must be.

With Empress Josephine held high, the doctor marched towards Madame Legrand. He would use them against her now. Piaf had to stop him. She slid nearer and attacked his shins and screamed holy war, each thump of her fist intensified by Luc and Bertie's hammering on the door.

Piaf clung to the doctor's leg, wrapping her own around it, desperate to stop him moving any closer to Madame. As though she were no more than a bicycle clip, he bore Piaf's full weight as he marched past Madame, elbowing the woman's face and shaking off Piaf as he turned suddenly to face one wooden dresser.

Behind his back, Piaf's fingers worked at great speed to release Madame from her ties, and, as Madame rose and swept her robe around Piaf, they witnessed the doctor do something very strange.

The man was walking slowly towards the closed dresser, singing and crying. He sounded hysterical, wired, manic. He held up Empress Josephine before him, like an offering, just as the barefoot man had done when he brought Rapiditus's Cabinet of Oils from Sainte-Chapelle to Notre-Dame on that busy, busy day. And, her memory flagged, just like the relic-carrying king in Sainte-Chapelle's stained window.

"They're a relic!" cried Piaf. "Empress Josephine is a relic!"

"That is a matter of opinion," muttered the doctor. "Are they merely a relic, or a magical key?"

Piaf heard the tinkle of small bottles vibrating around her. Luc peeked out from behind a wooden dresser, Bertie from another and the gentle click of thousands of insect feet on floorboards assured her she was fully surrounded. Piaf stalled the boys with a stare and pointed to the doctor.

Like peeling clouds from the sun, the doctor opened the double doors of the dresser. Everyone shielded their eyes from the glare that burst out, sending shards of reflected light across the apothecary until the dressers' lined-up bottles twinkled in reply. Squinting, Piaf saw it: a silver treasure chest with claw-shaped feet. The chest was no larger than a rich madame's jewellery box and was intricately carved with a maze of flailing crows and twisting snakes. She had seen it before, countless times, on the cover of *Le Petit Parisien* newspaper.

"Rapiditus's stolen Cabinet of Oils!" Piaf cried.

Piaf watched as the doctor ran his fingertips through the silver cabinet's wild, deep etchings. Then he held Empress Josephine flat and laid her gently on the cabinet's top.

Where the shape of Empress Josephine matched the cabinet's swirls, she sank down into its surface, and, with a gentle *clop*, she simply disappeared. Immediately, Piaf was reminded of the Grande Châsse and how the point where its lid met its base was imperceptible – not even a hairline crack. The

Cabinet of Oils and Empress Josephine were made for each other; the chest and its key were a perfect pair, like twins.

Piaf heard a snake-like hiss as the doctor raised the cabinet's now unlocked lid. He cleared his throat. "Madame Legrand, Chestnut Roaster, Véronique... and *friends*." He swirled each hand towards the dressers where Luc and Bertie failed to hide. "In approximately one hour this city will lose its light for the night..." He pulled one of two ancient glass bottles from the cabinet. Its green surface was cracked and pockmarked and, inside the bottle, an oil swirled. In the space between oil and cork, Piaf saw fog.

"The Oxygène! The forgetting fog!"

The doctor laughed. "*Forgetting fog* – I like that, though I am not sure Rapiditus would approve of such a... *simple* name for his genius. He had a reputation for performing miracles, quick as a flash – just like *that*." He snapped his fingers. "Or so it might have seemed."

Piaf immediately thought of the Miracles Parisiens – how people thought the Tour Eiffel had risen hundreds of feet and the colour of Notre-Dame had changed overnight. They had been tricked into believing a miracle had occurred by stripping them of memories – they'd lost a whole year.

"Whether you believe he was a saint or a magician, we can all agree Rapiditus was a man who relished the glory of *winning*, of *justice*, of *reputation*," preached the doctor. "So, I think he wouldn't mind sharing his techniques with me." The doctor checked his pocket-watch again. "By the power of Rapiditus's oil, everyone will lose their memories, again. WHAT OF IT? you all might ask, for they have already lost a year!" He laughed and tilted the bottle, as if to take stock of its dwindling contents. "This time, I am using more. Much more. It will set them back years. Enough time to throw this city into chaos. Enough time to delay their great plans. Enough time for justice to prevail." He looked into Véronique's eyes. "Enough time for us to win."

"Win *what*?" cried Madame.

The doctor seemed to snap out of his deep thought and returned the bottle of Oxygène to its cabinet with urgency. He grabbed the second bottle less gently. Piaf could see oil swirl inside this one too, but this time it was empty of any fog. The doctor quickly pulled out its cork with his teeth and spat it into the cabinet.

The smell of one hundred cherry berlingots washed across the room.

Piaf heard Luc's gasp. "The cure oil."

The doctor tapped the bottle against his pocket-watch and Piaf held her breath as he carelessly allowed droplets of precious oil fall to the floor with each *tap, tap, tap*. With each drop, a lost chance to recapture a lost memory.

The doctor beckoned Véronique. "Come, my daughter, this way."

"*My daughter?*" Piaf choked on her own words. The chained girl with the crooked nose, who he'd dragged from her roaster, was his *daughter?*

Véronique shuffled to her father's side.

"That's my girl. Everyone else might *lose* time but, with this, we will gain it." Between them, he poured a tiny pool of the bottle's cure oil into his palm.

Like a mad man, he smeared the sweet oil across his face in a layer thick as butter. It seemed a little went a long way as he wiped it into his clothes and used it to grease back his hair where the burr had tangled it. He turned Véronique's shoulders so that she was facing him and slapped it onto her sallow skin, each cold touch making her flinch and whimper.

"Don't fuss – you know this will protect your memory... weak as it is," he added under his breath. He caught himself and said, louder, "Shall I let you into a surprise, ma fille chérie?" His false smile was evident in his voice as he spoke to his daughter. "Papa *knew* you made that wooden chestnut burr for the Chestnut Roaster."

Véronique held her breath.

He smeared his daughter with more oil, until her cheeks shone red. "And Papa *knew* you made that leaf map. C'est magnifique – your best work. You have demonstrated that skill well." Whether on purpose or not, he stumbled on Véronique's wooden chestnut burr beneath his foot, smashing it into several pieces. "Papa is no fool." With one last drop placed gently on the tip of her crooked nose, he said, "But I forgive you. Because now we have our Chestnut Roaster exactly where we need her."

Piaf gasped. Madame wrapped her robe around Piaf tighter and pulled back.

The doctor turned to face Piaf and sniffed his sickly-sweet fingertips. "I would offer you some, but of course, you won't be needing it. When you answered my questions at your chestnut roaster, I *knew* I had finally found the right twin; the twin who can flick back through her memory like the pages of a thick book. The twin who cannot forget, even with the power of Rapiditus's oil, so it seems." He raised his head towards the dresser behind which Luc hid. "Master Luc, feel free to try Rapiditus's cure, but I fear it will do little but improve your complexion. I wouldn't have experimented so deeply in your brain had I known I had the wrong twin – a little girl! Who'd have thought it? Again, my apologies, but Madame Legrand..." he turned to face Madame, "your description was not very clear."

Piaf felt Madame's every muscle tense. "Don't listen to him," said Madame. "He's a liar." Piaf could see her jaw clench.

"*Liar?*" The doctor walked right up to them and took Madame by surprise when he suddenly held the bottle of sweet cure oil beneath Madame's nose – long enough for its fumes to pluck one memory from its slumber.

"Oh, ma plume," said Madame as her memory reshuffled. "It *was* me who told him about you. He came to Pufont's to have new buttons sewn onto his coat. He was telling me about how his studies on the

Cabinet of Oils were going, how it had something to do with *memory*. I told him all about you – my dear friend, the Chestnut Roaster, the twin who could never forget." She squinted her watering eyes. "Trust *him* to assume such a magnificent gift and burden could only be borne by a boy."

"Au contraire," said the doctor. "Quite the opposite." He carelessly tossed the bottle with its precious cure onto the round table. "I believe girls can be just as gifted as boys, even this one," he said and turned to face his daughter, "with the right help." He held his daughter's chin in his stinking hand. "For goodness' sake, *smile*, Véronique," he said. "We have found your final missing piece! The girl who cannot forget!" He scrubbed his oily hands together as a surgeon would do before cutting someone open, and lunged at Piaf.

Thirty-six | Trente-six

Through the raging folds of Madame's robe, Piaf saw flashes of Luc getting tangled up in the knot they had all become. He tugged at Dr Le Chandelier, trying to detach the man's hands from Piaf's hair. Piaf kicked and screamed and flapped. Madame pulled her hard, the doctor pulled her harder, she was spun and pinched and scratched until Madame relented for fear of snapping her in two.

The doctor stomped Luc away with his boot and picked Piaf up in his claw-like hands. He shook her, violently. "STOP. STOP FIGHTING IT, CHILD." Piaf stilled, and, like feeding scraps to a feral cat, he flicked her from a height into the hard chair.

The straps pinched and stung as he secured her to the arms of the chair. Blood poured from her nose. She begged for Maman, she kicked and squirmed but, no more than a bird trapped in a cage, could she escape.

Madame, Luc and Bertie slowly closed in, arms held out and eyes wild, surrounding the madman in a wide circle. Piaf knew they did not know what to do.

With a heaving chest, the doctor ran his hands through his tossed hair before fighting with the catch of a large leather bag sitting on the round table. As it opened, the glass bottle of Rapiditus's cure tipped over and a big droplet of oil bulged out, then another, and another, until it pooled on the table.

The cure was being wasted.

Piaf coughed and stared straight into Luc's eyes. *Read my mind like twins do. Get it, Luc, save the oil!* she wished with all her might.

Luc took a small step towards it.

The doctor thrashed about in the bag's contents until he found the scalpel he was looking for. He looked at Piaf, and she noticed him hold a breath. If only for a second, something had registered with him. He *saw* it – the damage he had done: blood from her nose trailing down her clothes, her lip swelling larger than before, scratches criss-crossing her arms, bruises already darkening the skin around her wrists.

When he dipped his head, he could see part of her coat beneath his boot. He peeled it away and began to laugh, or cry; Piaf could not tell.

He spun to face Luc, then Madame and Bertie. "DON'T COME ANY CLOSER!" He held the scalpel higher. "IT DIDN'T HAVE TO BE LIKE THIS!" he roared. His hands shook as he seemed to calm a bit. "All I need is your ability, child. I will not *take* it from you, I merely want you to share it." He turned and stared at his daughter. "Because what good is learning all the knowledge in the world if you cannot remember it?" Disappointment dampened every word.

The room went silent, but for the slow drip of the glass bottle's cure.

"Papa is right," said Véronique. She spoke so quietly and so sadly, they all turned and listened. "I let him down. I can't remember it all." She was standing with her back to them, at the dresser with its Cabinet of Oils. On a shelf above its double doors, her gentle fingertips ran along the labels of a row of twenty small glass bottles. "This small bottle holds something huge – the *Mathematics* of ten-year-old Faye Géraldine. Faye is brilliant," she said. "Her workings blew my mind, but I cannot remember one tenth of it now."

She moved her fingers to the next bottle in line. "This one here is *Music* by Dax Libraire—"

"Dax!" said Piaf. "The boy who could sing like an angel! Maman told me he went missing when he was carol singing." She saw Véronique nodding. Piaf stared at the doctor but he wouldn't look her in the eye and, instead, hurriedly lined up a concoction of medicines and surgical tools on the table before him.

Véronique wiped away her tears before she moved onto the next bottle. "*Dance*, my favourite essence, by Robere Colin." As though no one could see her, she raised her chin, arms and one leg and spun in a beautiful pirouette, just as she had done at the roaster.

Piaf's mind also spun. The leaf skeleton's tiny symbol of ballet shoes danced across her mind. The musical symbol, and abacus too. Each symbol and each bottle, a gifted child. Her skin prickled in shock: the doctor had harvested each child's gift, and captured it in a small glass bottle.

Véronique tapped her finger on the next label in line. "That is your gift, Bertrand Pufont." Véronique nudged the toe of her shoe to the right until it met with her smashed-up wooden burr.

Bertie shuddered.

"With your talent, Papa was sure I would win."

Win? Piaf gasped when a memory box whispered something in her ear. "The Exposition Universelle!" Piaf cried. She pointed at the doctor. "You want your daughter to win the Enfants Surdoués Showcase! You want her to be the most gifted child in the world. Is that why you did this? Is that what you want?" She was taken aback when the doctor's face bloomed red.

"Oui," said Véronique, her soft voice suddenly edged with sharpness. "But Papa says *one coin does not make a rich man*, so he gave me the gifts of every child who'd been accepted into the competition – all twenty of them."

"Mon Dieu, why would you do that to your own child?" hissed Madame.

Véronique turned to face Madame. "Madame Legrand, I am weak, *incomplète*. I am no good."

Dr Le Chandelier let a vial drop from his hand. It smashed to pieces between his boots. Though it was empty, it had the effect of a magic potion: the man almost seemed to shrink where he stood, shoulders slumped, head and heart down.

Piaf heard the wobble in Véronique's sigh as she continued, "Papa wanted to 'fix' me, so he force-fed my mind like he was fattening a goose. *Physics, Divination, Medicine, Poetry*, every gift you can think of..." She ran her finger quickly along the last few labels and stopped at the last one. She tapped its cork, light as a feather. "Most recently, *Zoolingualism*—"

"The power to communicate with beasts big and small," explained Luc.

"That is right," said Véronique, with a sharp nod. "A brilliant gift. They were *all* brilliant gifts. But, as the weeks went by, I began to forget them. I do not have a memory like yours, Chestnut Roaster, so Papa insisted on one last gift – your mind." She turned to face her father, her voice stronger than before. "But I am sorry, Papa, we are NOT going to win. We are not going to win because these..." she swung her hand behind her and knocked all twenty bottles to the ground, "... these gifts were never your gifts to give." And that was when the quiet girl with the crooked nose opened her mouth, wide as a lion, and roared.

Véronique summoned the rats that had chased Piaf to invade the apothecary. She raised her hand, directing them like Mother Nature until they rose like a tsunami towards her father. Another roar brought a torrent of bats; they swirled around the room, smashing bottles to the floor and, when they were done, they snuffed out the candles' flames, one by one, until the room faded from amber to grey to black.

Blinded by darkness, Piaf kicked and yelled as ants, beetles and cockroaches squirmed beneath her bare feet in a layer thick as quicksand. Véronique's voice smashed through the chaos, sending the fox hurtling towards the doctor.

The fox's jaws snapped; the doctor yelled. The fox's jaws snapped again. And again, until the doctor's yells sank to a growl, then a whimper. He was hurt.

Piaf tried with all her might to set herself free of the chair's leather straps. "HELP! I'M STUCK!" she roared. Within seconds she felt the gentle pull at the leather on her wrists. Blinded, her mind filled in the picture – were rats nibbling her way to freedom? Her left hand flew up as it snapped free, and she made a grab for her other wrist. Instead of a rat, she felt the gentle, oily fingertips of a girl. They clasped hands.

"Véronique?"

The fox yelped; a blood-curdling cry of pain.

"Please stop my Papa," was all Véronique said. Piaf heard the rattling of Véronique's chain before the girl with the crooked nose was, once again, dragged away.

"CATCH HIM!" roared Piaf. Flying insects flicked at her skin. She reached out in the dark, treading on creatures, slapping bats' wings with her hands. The screams of humans and beasts, glass smashing and dressers falling, filled the room. She felt like she was climbing and climbing or falling and falling until, like a slap to the face, there was light.

The chaos around her dropped down like autumn leaves from a tree.

She was leaning against the round table, panting. The doctor and his daughter were gone.

Twelve knights of the Order of the Holy Sepulchre had arrived. They were shuffling into a perfect circle around her, lamps held high above their heads. Luc, Bertie and Madame joined them.

Piaf turned slowly on the spot. They were all staring down at her with a look in their eyes she did not immediately recognise. They were silent, they were ready, and they were waiting.

It dawned on her: they were on her side.

The grouchy knight from Sainte-Chapelle took a limped step forward. "Piaf Durand, Chestnut Roaster of Rue du Dragon, tell us what to do."

Thirty-seven | Trente-sept

Like the closed petals of a flower bud, the twelve knights hunched around the round table, hurriedly syringing up the pool of cure oil. Bertie and Madame, with the help of Véronique's loyal rats and the doctor's strange gloves, scavenged hundreds of unbroken bottles and their tiny corks from the floor's layer of crushed glass. All as Piaf had instructed.

"Each bottle needs just a single drop," said Bertie as he delivered another handful to the round table. "It should be enough to bring back everyone's memory in an instant – the air will react with it and send it up to the Overground through entonnoirs."

"Each missing child will have made at least twenty or thirty of these entonnoirs," warned Piaf, as she unfurled the leaf skeleton from her finger. "And you will need one bottle for each, so carry as many as you can. Rescue the children first, restore their memories, and they will then help place the bottles under their entonnoirs out there. Be sure to remove the cork before you move on."

"You can use your cloaks' hoods to hold the bottles," suggested Madame as she demonstrated with her own.

Piaf looked down upon the leaf between her fingers. Though delicate and small, it was entirely unscathed, perfect as the moment she had first set eyes on it.

It didn't need to be big and strong to survive.

She quickly passed it to Luc who held it steady over the grouchy knight's lamp. Luc looked up at its shadow, but suddenly dropped his hands.

"Déjà vu, I've been here before," he said. He pointed up to a small square hole in the apothecary ceiling where the neat wood panels gave way to crudely nailed slats of wood. Hundreds of bats hung around it like giant raindrops, watching the seething action below. "That's a trap door," he said, "and it leads up to the Jardin des Tuileries' tallest chestnut tree."

"Where I found you," said Piaf. "The day you lost your memory."

Luc glanced at the strap of Piaf's bag, "I remember falling through that hole. The doctor smothered me with his Oxygène soon as I fell – it was on a rag. I tried to call to the ghost girl – Véronique – but I couldn't breathe." Piaf watched as he pulled at the skin on his face.

Piaf placed a hand on his arm, her touch asking a very important question: could he remember more now? Could he remember his life? The cure oil's scent of one hundred cherry berlingots was so strong in the room, Piaf could feel it seep into every pore.

"No," said Luc, sadly, and he cast the map's shadow once more.

Piaf's heart sank. He *still* could not remember. While she'd handed out instructions, she'd watched him smell that cure oil, straight from the cabinet's bottle, until his eyes cried, and yet, unlike Madame and Bertie, he could not remember his life before the day he'd fallen ill. Perhaps the doctor was not lying when he'd said he might have dug a little too deep.

"There are nineteen children out there," said Luc.

Piaf urgently scooped several filled glass bottles of cure oil into her bag. "We have no time to waste."

The bats seemed to flutter in response, making the map's shadow shimmer like sunlight on the Seine.

Someone tapped Piaf's shoulder.

"Grouchy Knight!" said Piaf, then swiftly apologised.

The knight's hood clinked with bottles as he smiled and nodded, seemingly happy with his new title. "I am ready," he said, and turned to Luc. "But I fear I am a little slow – can you direct me to the nearest entonnoirs, please?" Another knight lined up behind him.

"Thank you for your help," said Piaf, her eyes asking a million questions, most of them beginning with why? The knights at Notre-Dame had clearly not been on her side as they and the doctor chased her through the crowds.

The knight placed a hand on his chest. "As have all my brothers for their wards, I have given my life to protect my dear, dear Sainte-Chapelle." Piaf was not surprised at how he spoke of the chapel like it were family. "She is my life. We are joined at the hip," he said and patted his leg and moaned. Piaf caught him as he stumbled.

"I always slept better on the nights you took refuge in her, if even for a few hours. I knew she would come to no harm because I saw the love you have for her in your eyes – that smile on your face when you thought I wasn't watching, that joy in your whispers as you hid in her stairwell. I'm quite sure my chapel's walls would smile, too, as you sang, and the stars in her ceiling would twinkle while you played king and queen." He tightened the clasp of his sword's scabbard as though he were ready for action. "I knew you would leave her unharmed, even as you hid inside the Grande Châsse itself."

Piaf's eyes opened wide. "You knew we were in there?"

For the first time ever, Piaf saw a smile grace the grouchy knight's lips.

"I trusted you," he said, proudly. "They accused you of being a criminal, and when Knight Vecchio told me you'd announced to the world that Saint Rapiditus's Cabinet of Oils had been stolen, I dug a little deeper. I despise paperwork," he moaned. "But I checked my records, and those of Notre-Dame's Treasury, and found evidence of the cabinet's disappearance – *a whole year ago!*" The table of knights turned, shaking their heads in both disbelief and agreement.

"Every day of the year stolen from our minds was

documented," he continued. "We have been searching for you and the doctor ever since." He patted Piaf's shoulder as if to say well done, straightened himself stiff as a soldier, and turned his attention to Luc and the map.

"Now, where are you sending me?" He moaned again when a bat flew down and hung from his wide sleeve.

Madame brought an unlit candle over to Piaf and peered down the dark tunnel to Piaf's left. "Ma petite plume, I am not happy for you to go out there alone." But she knew not to try stopping her as Maman would have done. Though a plan was in action to rescue the children and restore the memories of all of Paris, Piaf could not allow the doctor to simply disappear like Bertie's ghost of Philibert Aspairt, at least not as long as Véronique was chained to him.

Madame hugged her tight and kissed the top of her head. "We will come find you once everyone has been saved."

Piaf held the wick of her candle to the lamp's flame beneath the leaf in Luc's hands. As she waited for it to take hold, she instinctively rose on her tiptoes beside him. They were silent for a moment, then Luc looked at her and used his elbows to push her back onto the flat of her feet. "I might have to look down at you, Piaf, but I will always look up to you. That's a fact."

The flame split in two and, feeling infinitely braver, she walked away.

She took one last look at everyone in the apothecary and the army they had all become. Memory boxes took their places and quietened, watching and waiting for the show to begin. It was time for her to go.

Piaf ran to the one open door where Véronique's loyal and injured fox stood; tail straight, eyes sharp, nose catching the fading scent of the doctor and his daughter. *This way*, it was saying. Piaf patted its head, and ran and ran and ran.

Thirty-eight | Trente-huit

The Main Vein, The River Seine, Paris

Piaf had been running along the main vein of the map for some time before she came to a halt, desperate to catch her breath and banish the aching stitch in her side. Next to her, a flat stone jutted out from the tunnel's wall. It was almost like a washbasin, and rainwater filtered by rock splashed down upon it, each drip loud as a smack. On her tiptoes, she twisted her body, shut her eyes tight and caught droplets on her cracked tongue. A memory of twirling to catch falling snowflakes with Maman bulged in her mind, and it quickly awakened another, reminding her that

Maman was helping the doctor, but, to her surprise, her mind settled again.

Somehow, it had been shushed.

You can do this, her mind ushered instead.

One more drop, and she was satisfied. She opened her eyes, ready to race on, but something caught her attention. She turned around and scanned the tunnel's wall with her candlelight.

Something glistened.

"Blood!" she cried. Her word and her horror echoed on and on, and so too did the bloody handprints smeared along the dry stone of the tunnel's wall. The handprints would fade to almost nothing and then reappear, bloodier than ever. The fox had left its mark on the doctor, and it didn't take much for Piaf to imagine the man grasping at his injury and then using the wall for support.

She would catch him soon.

She ran on at a pace, fast as the candle's flame would allow. The tunnel was long and straight, only a few turns to the left and even fewer to the right. Blood-stained letters etched into the stone walls had told her what stood above: the *Arc de Triomphe*, then *Louvre*, and further along, *Les Halles* – she was following the flow of the Seine back towards the river's island: Île de la Cité. But it wasn't the blood that told her to turn right at a sign for *Pont Neuf* – it was the rushed, yet definite arrow dragged by the heel of a small shoe into the dusty ground that told her so. *Véronique.*

The narrow tunnel dropped down into a dangerous, muddy slope before her, sometimes resorting to jagged stone steps. Feathered green slime coated the walls. The air changed too. Her stomach retched. She felt like she was climbing into the gut of a monster. She held her candle out before her and something flashed back: there was water ahead.

"NO, PAPA! NO!"

Véronique's voice pummelled down the black tunnel towards Piaf, snagging her like a claw, and pulling her into the shockingly cold water without a second's thought. Knee deep, then hip level, the stale and stagnant remains of the raging river above deepened and deepened. Piaf did not care, but the candle hissed in despair. She held it higher and higher and used her free hand to leverage herself along as the water climbed up her chest and met with her chin.

Soon, her feet had no choice but to abandon the ground, and she hung from the roof of the tunnel itself where cracks wide enough to take her fingers allowed a steady grip. River water from above trickled down, splashing into her eyes and filling her mouth, threatening with every gained inch to snuff out her only source of light.

Her arm muscles burned, her torn skin stung, the gap between water and roof shrank and shrank.

She was in real danger, and the boxes in her mind heaved and bellowed with every breath she took. *Keep going*, they cried. An image of Pont Neuf bridge flapped like a flag, telling her that overhead were its seven arches and soon, at the bridge's centre point, they would meet the tip of Île de la Cité where the island's land rose to greet it.

The water level will drop, her memory promised, and so it did. The floor of the tunnel rose up and up to a dry, dusty platform no larger than her corner on Rue du Dragon.

Her chest burned with each breath, every muscle ached, but she was on dry ground more than halfway across the width of the river. She looked down. Two lines in the dust beneath her feet disappeared into the next tunnel before her – Véronique had been dragged.

Piaf held the candle up and took a few steps down into the remaining stretch of tunnel. Though only five more arches stood overhead, the tunnel beneath them was deeper and narrower than before. Her feet slipped in Véronique's tracks. A line of hot wax seared her cheek as she slid down and down until the strap of her bag caught on a rock. Inches from the water's edge, her stomach flipped.

The reason for Véronique's yell was clear: the tunnel was completely submerged.

Piaf swung her bag behind her back and licked her fingers to pinch out the flame.

Blackness.

You'll be the death of me, Maman's voice bubbled in her mind.

She took a deep breath and dived in.

Piaf kicked, she swung her arms, every muscle and bone right down to her fingertips and toes fought against the tunnel's water. She kept at it and kept at it, until panic rose: was she moving, or stalled on the spot? Where was up? Where was down?

She was too weak! Too small! Her arms flailed; her courage too.

Keep going, her memory boxes roared and roared, so she tried even harder. As she scooped her way through, the largest box dominated her mind. It flipped its lid and, as she fought for her life, the box flicked out the memories crammed inside:

How she'd stood up to that stranger at her roaster;

How she'd coped with the illness, and loss, of her brother – living his nightmare as though it were her own;

How she'd helped Maman through the timeless dark days after Papa's death;

How her own heart was for ever bruised;

How she'd kept their roaster – their future – going;

And how she'd stood tall against her fears.

You can do it, the boxes cheered, *You can do it*. She swam stronger.

Her memory sped up: how she'd tackled the crowds and evaded capture at Notre-Dame, *flick;* how she'd helped Bertie, *flick;* how she'd escaped through the terrifying tunnels of Paris's underground twin, *flick;* how she'd spoken to an army of knights and friends, *fearlessly*, and how they'd listened.

Nearly there. Pin pricks stabbed her lungs as the last of her breath whittled away. Her left elbow scraped along a rock. Her right arm too. She grabbed the walls of the narrowing tunnel and propelled herself through faster and faster until the ground rose and struck her knees. She crawled her way out of the water and opened her eyes.

Blackness. Air, far fresher than before, swept over her wet skin. Shivers rushed through her and she rubbed heat into her arms with the wrinkled flesh of her fingers. Unable to see, she lost balance and swung her arms out wide, moving them slowly in a protective bubble. The silence weighed heavy in her ears and made her breath as deafening as a passing carriage, her pulse loud as horses' hooves. She blinked water from her lashes and stared hard again.

"Light!" she whispered. Ahead, the faintest hint of blue light hazed the air, shaping the tunnel before her. She shuffled her feet forward until bravery kicked them into walking, then running. Brighter and brighter the haze became until she came to a stop at an entonnoir.

She looked up, and gasped. She was far closer to the ground than she'd expected, the hole much wider than before. There was still daylight out there, but a star was just visible against the blue.

Night was falling.

As she swung her dripping bag back around to her stomach, her memory took over and she was suddenly back in the chatière of Bertie's nest listening to the doctor. "Stand back when you remove the cork," he had said. She placed the bottle of cure oil directly beneath the entonnoir and pinched and pulled at its cork with her broken nails until it released with a quiet pop.

She watched as the rush of cold air from above hooked a thin finger of the strange, see-through gas swirling out of the bottle. Looking through it, the shiny veins in the rock glistened, the buttery stone shone richer. Like Aladdin's genie, the swirling gas grew wider and wider with every inch before disappearing up the shaft with a whoosh.

She ran on as far as the fading light allowed and, just as she slowed to meet with a wall of complete darkness, another haze of blue light appeared in the distance. On she ran, from entonnoir to entonnoir, only slowing to catch her breath when her last bottle of cure oil was placed. Where was the doctor? Where was Véronique? She scanned the walls, praying for a sign – blood, even – anything that would lead her to them.

A sudden bang, loud as overhead thunder, shrank her down into a ball. She wrapped her arms around her head and rolled onto her side. Dust coated her mouth and gritted her eyes and she waited for pain to arrive. When it didn't, and the world beneath her feet settled, she moved. Like she was uncurling the leaf skeleton, she gently stretched herself out and stood, fragile yet strong, and stared down at an enormous rock. It had crashed to the floor, missing her head by inches.

She looked up at the black hole from where the rock had fallen. A crack crawled out of it like a rat's black tail, and her blood froze in her veins as the jagged line slowly crept across the ceiling and down the wall. The ground beneath her trembled, the walls shook. She ran and ran, as the crack and its cloud of dust chased her.

She came to a sudden stop.

She was in a cave with its rough, spiky walls. The space appeared untouched by man, but for the ceiling, which was pockmarked with a glut of entonnoirs.

Beneath them, in the centre of the room, was a large slab of rock – a ledger stone, marking the grave of an ancient lost soul. And on it, surrounded by a frame of etched letters, lay a broken man in the arms of his daughter.

Thirty-nine | Trente-neuf

Rapiditus's Tomb,
Beneath Rue du Dragon, Paris

Jagged cracks in the cave walls snapped and slapped like an audience while, centre-stage, the doctor writhed in pain and his daughter wept into her hand.

"Véronique!" said Piaf. She took a step towards them, suddenly unsure what to do.

"Papa is hurt," Véronique cried. Piaf stared as the girl unhooked her chain from her injured father's wrist and ran her hands over the deep crevices of his face.

He jolted at her touch.

His eyes opened and he saw Piaf.

"Chestnut Roaster," he said, his voice cracked and weak. His bloodied hands slowly formed a fist; spit bubbled from between his gritted teeth. Véronique swiped her hands away when the lines on his face tightened. He tried to rise, as though to finish something he had started, only to collapse back down.

Véronique pressed down on his shoulders. "No, Papa!" The ground shook, chips of mud and stone rained down through hazy blue entonnoir light.

Piaf approached him and stared down at the gash in his side. Though blood had turned his clothes black, it was not to blame for the pain he was feeling.

"I know what it is like," said Piaf, "when bad memories rage inside your mind." She was surprised at how confident her words sounded.

The doctor closed his eyes and seemed to breathe in her words deeply, so she continued. "I know what it is like when, no matter how hard you try, you cannot forget. Especially if you have done something you regret."

The doctor slowly nodded. "*Tourmenté*," he whispered. "I cannot bear it anymore."

Piaf watched Véronique hugging him tight, just as Piaf would hug Maman and just as she once hugged her own Papa. She felt her own thinking reshuffle: she could see the love Véronique had for her Papa despite all he had done – there was more to this man than a villain.

"A chestnut," said Piaf, "has a hard outside. It's tough, it's mean, it's even dangerous. And it hurts if you touch it. It wants you to fear it, but only because it fears you will hurt what's hidden deep inside. It wants to protect."

The doctor held his breath.

To her astonishment, a tear formed in the hollow next to his eye. He looked up at his daughter and, as life itself began to slip away, so too did the cold hard mask of a wicked man. "I am sorry, ma fille brillante," he said most softly. "I failed you." He clamped his teeth shut as pain coursed through him.

When he tried to say more, Véronique's fingertips pressed against his lips. "Papa, don't speak." She could see the toll each word was having on him.

"I think your Papa wants to confess," Piaf said gently, and she understood why – it would help settle the regrets he clearly had.

Véronique inched closer to her father and raised his head onto her knees.

"*Exposition Universelle,*" he said. For a split second, Piaf was sure she could see stars in his red-lined eyes. "Where the great minds of the world are celebrated – young and old. When the exposition's committee refused to register you, my brilliant daughter, for the Enfants Surdoués Showcase— HOW DARE THEY," he seethed and grabbed at his wound, "I did what was right. I found the list of entrants. One child – that was all I chose – one gifted child; a mathematician."

"Her name was Faye Géraldine," said Véronique.

The doctor's face crumpled. Shame seemed to ooze from every pore. "When I saw the terror in the young mathematician's face, I *had* to help her. I *had* to do something that would make her forget what I had done. One small drop of Rapiditus's oil was all I needed." He reached down and ran his fingers over the etched letters of the stone slab beneath him.

"*Rapiditus,*" Piaf read. They were at his tomb. Her imagination flashed a picture of his crumbling bones below the stone.

The doctor's hands curled inwards as pain gripped him tight. "I would have let the girl go! Go back to her family! But— AGH!" Every muscle tightened; Véronique wept.

"But Véronique couldn't remember all the knowledge she had gained," continued Piaf.

"I had to repeat the procedure, and, each time, I needed another drop of Rapiditus's oil. Then I got greedy."

"He could not stop," whispered Véronique. "He took child after child."

"Madame Legrand," he said, his words curling his lips down into an ugly line. "We... shall we say 'ran into each other' underground. She was carrying spices and a bag of buttons," he said. "I was carrying an unconscious child." He began to laugh, the kind of laugh that meant he knew it was far from funny.

"That night, Madame followed me. All the way to Notre-Dame. She saw me siphon another drop of Rapiditus's oil from the Cabinet of Oils. I was stealing it, drop by drop. She raged war against me," he said, and Piaf could believe it. "She screamed that she had already told the police of the unconscious child. That they would catch me. We struggled over the Cabinet of Oils as I ran with it – she is a strong woman, but she fell, tripped, I think. She was hurt – concussed, I determined, and she remained unconscious. The cabinet's key was hidden beneath her—"

"Empress Josephine," said Piaf.

"The cabinet was open. I did not need it."

"Until I closed it," said Véronique, quietly.

"My plans were failing. The Exposition was only months away. I needed more time to prepare you," he squeezed his daughter's hand, "and I could not risk getting caught."

"So you poisoned the city," said Piaf. As if in reply, deep fissures shot up the cave's walls like fireworks.

Dr Le Chandelier stared up at his daughter. "I only wanted to help you – help you to succeed, as I have succeeded, and just as my father before me and his father before him had to succeed. Your ancestor made sure of that."

"*Ancestor?* Papa?"

"Rapiditus." The doctor spat every syllable with hatred and blood. "He set in stone the INSUFFERABLE standards his descendants must aspire to meet. People marvelled when the great Rapiditus somehow rose from a commoner to a nobleman, and even a saint, *overnight*, casting miracles as he conquered and bewildered," he said, anger tingeing his pale face red. "But I'm no fool – I knew Rapiditus's power and his miracles were down to more than hard work. The legend of his Cabinet of Oils was proven when they were rediscovered, and I was determined to discover what part they played in his unquenchable desire to be the best." The doctor flicked a look at Piaf. "Just as I am sure your memory is a burden to you, Chestnut Roaster, so too is my family's inherited ambition to achieve. It is TORTURE."

Piaf stayed silent when the doctor paused to catch his breath. He grasped his daughter's hand, his words weaker now. "So, my dear Véronique, when you were born, I knew the horrendous struggle that lay before you to achieve such expected greatness. But, as you grew, I wanted the world to see you for what you truly are. To recognise how perfect and brilliant you are. Alas, you were *entirely* invisible to them." He raised a trembling hand towards his daughter's face, and gently closed her eyelids. "They were blinded by your blindness, my dear, dear Véronique."

Piaf gasped. She stared at Véronique. "You are blind?" Her eye jumped to the small chain dangling from Véronique's wrist as the girl wiped away a tear

– the chain was there to protect and guide her, not restrain her.

The ground rumbled; several rocks fell from the roof of the cave. Like the world had been dropped from a height, Piaf's body jerked downwards, the sound of cracks slapped against her ears. She stared up at the ceiling; the light from the glut of entonnoirs flickered.

Fontis! Fontis! Sinkholes! flapped Piaf's memory. They were in the sixth arrondissement! Bertie's numerous entonnoirs had weakened the foundations just as the doctor had warned him. There was only one thing worse than standing above a sinkhole, and that was standing beneath one.

"WE NEED TO GO!" cried Piaf. She tugged at Véronique, but she was stiff as stone.

Beneath the girl and her father, Rapiditus's ledger stone cracked in two. Véronique's fingers were on her father's lips and Piaf watched them move as he spoke one last time: "Au revoir."

Only then, did Véronique collapse into Piaf's arms.

Piaf swooped her away, and they ran and ducked as rock rained down like the Great Leonid Meteor

Storm of 1833, exploding as they hit the ground around them.

Backed up against the cave's wall, Piaf turned and watched as the floor beneath the doctor began to crumble. As tall as the Tour Eiffel rose to the sky, a chasm just as deep opened up beneath them. Dr Le Chandelier and all his regrets, along with the bones of old Rapiditus, had disappeared.

As they ran through a rip in the cave wall, Piaf's memory pounded in panic: falling down sinkholes, down, down, past rock and bone, and she swore she saw flashes of a crumpled chestnut roaster. Once more there was dust and sharp edges, grit between her teeth, and a thudding and rumbling, deep as thunder. She pushed Véronique into a narrow alcove, her cries silenced by the roar of falling stone. Beneath the alcove's single entonnoir, Véronique fell to the ground.

She was broken, cracked, and curled into a ball like a delicate egg. Like feathered wings, Piaf wrapped her arms around Véronique as the girl's world fell apart and a wall of rocks fell before them.

They were trapped.

Piaf had no idea how long they stayed like that. A

memory box, dedicated to the loss of her own Papa, had softly floated forward, helping Piaf wrap her new friend with words of comfort. Véronique listened to every word.

"Can you forgive me?" Véronique finally said, wiping her tears away with her palms. "Papa was right, I *lured* you to his apothecary." Piaf recalled the floating light they'd seen at the first entonnoir and the strange noises that had pulled her through the tunnels like a carrot before a horse. She wondered if she were looking at Bertie's ghost too – the one he could feel staring at him through dark tunnels. "I knew from how Papa spoke of your power that only you would be able to save us."

Before Piaf could reply, Véronique seemed to sense something Piaf could not. "They have come!" she said. Seconds later, through clearing clouds of dust, a bat squeezed through a gap between fallen rocks and swooped and clapped its wings overhead. Shouts, urgent footsteps and the clink of glass followed; their army of friends were on their way.

Piaf helped Véronique to her feet.

She squeezed thanks into Piaf's hand. "May I *see* you, Chestnut Roaster?" Just as she had read her suffering father's face, Véronique's fingertips reached up high as the sky to read Piaf's.

Piaf frowned and reached up to lower the girl's hands. "I'm down here," she said with a smile.

"Oh," said Véronique. "I thought you were a giant."

Forty | Quarante

Piaf's Corner, Rue du Dragon, Paris

Piaf climbed her way out of the sinkhole on her corner of Rue du Dragon.

As she had done the moment she was born, she stretched each limb out, one at a time, and she took the deepest breath of cool, slightly sweetened, October 1888 air.

She stood there for a moment, dishevelled, alive and elated.

Through hundreds of entonnoirs, life in the overground city was being transformed. But there was no fog this time. Like thumb-rubbing breath from a windowpane, everything around her appeared clearer and crisper as Rapiditus's miraculous cure polished the air. She looked up. The stars in the sky were bright as snowflakes, far brighter than she had ever seen before. Oil-lamps swaying on passing carriages bright as sunbeams. The air felt so fresh she could feel it fold around her arms, her bare feet, her scratched cheeks, even her scalp where her matted hair pulled tight. Sounds blossomed around her too, deeper and higher: the *swish* of the wind, the *crunch* of dust underfoot, a distant mouse scratching, disturbed swifts screeching. Voices near and far rang out like the keys of a grand piano.

Something else felt different, too.

Though she hadn't grown an inch, she felt taller than before.

She turned in a slow circle, gulping up every bit of the Overground. It was late at night, and it was cold, but every shop and every café was open, *bustling*, every window bright with light, every front door ajar. On street corners and doorways, she could see people jump with glee or crumple to the ground, and sometimes both, as they breathed in the sweet, cherry berlingot scented air, replenishing lost memories of the year; a year's worth of celebrations and loss, joyous

319

days and sad times, good decisions and bad, wishes come true, shocks, surprises and loving moments all felt again.

All in an instant.

A crowd began to form across the road outside Pufont's Button Bijouterie. As though Piaf was centre-stage at L'Opéra de Paris, the men, women and children faced her and her corner, staring and clapping as news of her leadership and her bravery spread as far and wide as the cure had flown.

"Piaf!"

Piaf spun around and peered back down into Paris's underground twin. Luc was down there, helping Véronique climb up. Piaf reached low and grabbed her hand. Véronique squeezed it tight as she took her last steep step, and something hard dug into Piaf's palm.

"Ouch! What *is* that?"

"Squirrels," said Véronique, as she found her footing. "It feels like three beautiful squirrels." She pressed it into Piaf's hand.

"You found my button!" Piaf's eyes searched for Bertie as the last of the cloaked knights and gifted children emerged from the sinkhole.

She wanted him to know she would sew the squirrel button to the *outside* of her coat.

She would no longer fear the power of her memory. When it mattered, it had saved her.

"Thank you," she whispered to her memory. She felt her words echoing down the squirming tunnels and alleyways of her mind, until they reached the millions of small wooden boxes that lived there. She smiled and stood proud. Like Luc had said, she had a *superpower*, after all.

She took Véronique's hand in hers and described the scene before them. Several police officers held back the growing crowd as it closed in, and soon Piaf's army of twelve knights and twenty gifted children surrounded her like rays of sunshine.

Cries of immense joy rang out as parents were reunited with their missing children, seeking out and pledging to thank the Chestnut Roaster for the rest of their lives before plucking their boys and girls away. As gaps appeared between knights, Piaf stood on her tiptoes, scanning the heaving crowd beyond.

At first, they all looked like strangers – like a flock of birds, she was unable to distinguish one from another. Then, Monsieur Auguste, waving from Les Deux Magots! And Monsieur Pufont walking towards Bertie, raising his hat in celebration! Piaf waved back and he put his hand on his heart. She began to recognise faces of her customers, every one of them smiling at her, blowing kisses. And finally, between the cloak of the grouchy knight and the police officer from Notre-Dame, she found the one person she was looking for.

Piaf froze to the spot.

Instantly, she felt Véronique's thumb gently stroking her hand, comforting. "Are you all right?" asked Véronique. Piaf realised she had squeezed her hand too tight.

"It's Maman."

"Ma petite Piaf!" Maman ran towards her, ducking and diving through the crowd and passers-by. Not once did she break eye-contact with Piaf. "Ma petite Piaf!" she cried again as she dropped to her knees before her daughter. Quick as lightning, Maman's eyes and her hands ran over every inch of Piaf. "Are you hurt? Did he hurt you?" She put her hand on Piaf's heart.

It felt like a soothing balm. Maman stood and

reached out her arm when Luc came running towards them and, in an instant, Maman knew his memory had not returned. Piaf was amazed at how Maman had restrained her instincts to smother him as she pulled him into a gentle hug – she was still a stranger to Luc, and it would take time.

As Maman spoke, Piaf thought her mother had never looked so fragile, like an exhausted bird failing to crack out from its shell. "Piaf, Luc, can you ever forgive me?" she finally begged. She had believed the doctor when he told her they were both gravely ill, that they needed his care or Maman would lose them forever. Maman did not know she was faced with the devil. She covered her face with her hands in shame. "Madame Legrand begged me to believe her – she told me everything that had happened in the asylum before you escaped. But I was so afraid." Piaf recalled how Madame had pulled her robe's hood across her own face to protect herself from the Oxygène fog in Luc's room. She had not forgotten what she witnessed, but Maman had.

Had Maman known what the doctor had done, she would have never, ever put them in harm's way. Not Maman.

Much to Piaf's surprise, she felt hot tears running down her own face and every doubt she ever had that Maman would knowingly help the doctor capture her, washed away. Véronique squeezed Piaf's hand – she had sensed it too.

"Luc!" cried Bertie, his voice bellowing from the sinkhole. Piaf could see the tip of something black bobbing up and down at the edge of the sinkhole. Luc smiled at Maman and left to help Bertie.

Maman hugged and hugged Piaf so tight the warmth and joy of it must have spread through her bones and into Véronique's, as it lit up her new friend's eyes and turned her cheeks pink. Maman would not let go and nor would Piaf until a whistle and a hearty laugh separated them. It was Madame Legrand, her smile so wide her one gold tooth sparkled in the moonlight.

"Rosetta!" Maman kissed her dear friend's cheeks but sprung back to wrap her arms around Piaf again. "I never want to let you go, ma petite Piaf."

Madame took Véronique's hand from Piaf's, whispered words in the girl's ear that appeared to pour comfort, and pulled her firmly under her wing. "You will stay with me, mon pétale."

"And please, Madame, tell me you will both stay with me and my grandson," said Monsieur Pufont. He looked at the several floors of balconied windows above the button shop. "Bertie and I find it a little lonely." He cleared his throat and his emotions and said, "Madame Legrand, I will retire soon, and Pufont's will have a bright future ahead of it with Bertie and, if I am to believe my grandson, Véronique's skills too." He took Madame's hand in his. "Will you please consider all that I have your own, Madame?" Before he could say another word, Madame straightened one of his buttons, smiled and squeezed enormous gratitude into his hand.

Everyone jumped as fireworks boomed overhead. Maman hugged Piaf even tighter.

"Oh, Marie, mon cherie!" said Madame to Maman as they looked to the stars. "We must always hold our dear children tight…" she rubbed kindness into Maman's shoulder, "…but we must be careful not to clip their wings! Oui?"

"Oui," said Maman. Piaf smiled when Maman cupped her warm hands around her daughter's face. "Why would I stop her, now that I know she can fly?" Maman smiled back and tried to ruffle Piaf's hair but her fingers got stuck. "Mon Dieu! Your hair! You'll be the death of me, Piaf Durand. Look at you!"

Another firework lit up the Overground with a flash of daylight.

"And look at me, too! Sacré bleu!" said Madame Legrand with a whistle. She shook the dried mud from her clothes. Her robe was colourless, and gone were her polished nails, her jewellery and silk scarf. "But it doesn't matter what is on the outside," she said, admiring the leaf skeleton on her finger as though it were a precious gem. "Isn't that right, ma plume?" she said to Piaf and winked.

Piaf instantly knew Madame wasn't just referring to her muddy robe. Nor was she referring to her imaginary grand château she had once thought important to the impression she created.

She was talking about Piaf.

It did not matter that she was so small, and to most, appeared fragile as a leaf skeleton.

What mattered was that, inside, Piaf was a giant.

"Piaf Durand, the Chestnut Roaster!" Piaf turned to see the grouchy knight limping his way towards her, his white robe glowing in the reflected light of the Cabinet of Oils which he cradled in his arms. "On behalf of the Order of the Holy Sepulchre, the Treasury of Notre-Dame and the Basilica of Our Lady of the Thorn in Évron, we thank you for rescuing the precious Cabinet of Oils of Saint Rapiditus, and for the discovery of the long-lost tomb of its creator."

An officer appeared at his side. "Knight Jeremiah, Mademoiselle Durand – we have searched the chasm where the tomb of Rapiditus and Dr Le Chandelier fell. We located the tomb, but…"

Véronique stepped out of Madame's hold. "Papa?"

The officer removed his helmet. "I am sorry, Mademoiselle Le Chandelier. Our initial examination of the chasm shows evidence of another complex network of tunnels, as large and impressive as the one above it. We will do everything we can to find him, Mademoiselle, but for now, there is no trace of your father. Disparu."

"Disappeared?" Piaf reached out for Véronique's hand. They had both witnessed her father's injuries. "There is no way he could've escaped. It would take a miracle."

The grouchy knight's face suddenly paled, white

as his robe. "The oils of Saint Rapiditus… c'est incomplète!" He lifted the lid of the silver cabinet.

Piaf peered in. On the left side of the cabinet stood the bottle of the doctor's Oxygène – the forgetting fog. In the middle, the last of Rapiditus's cure. To its right, a gap.

Piaf gulped. "A bottle is missing?" The knight nodded. "What was in it?"

"We do not know. Already my brothers are urgently studying the history of Saint Rapiditus and his mysterious miracles. That and his tomb might provide some answers." He looked down into the sinkhole and down into the black chasm below that again. "Time will tell."

Everyone turned and stared at Véronique.

Madame flicked everyone away with her hand and shrouded Véronique in the folds of her robe. "Véronique, mon pétale – let us go home." They turned to walk away.

"Piaf. Will I see you tomorrow?" asked Véronique. She offered a little smile.

"I'll be right here," said Piaf. "On my corner. Where we first met." Véronique waved goodbye and Piaf watched them go. A niggling memory box tickled her mind. "Véronique! Wait! What happened to your nose?" The box that had hung about patiently from the moment she'd seen the girl with the crooked nose, finally settled with a sigh.

"Luc," said Véronique, with a big smile. "Luc happened."

"That's a fact," said Luc from behind. Piaf spun around to face him. In his arms was a pile of broken chestnut-roaster wood. Bertie, standing next to him, held a wheel under each arm. "It is my earliest memory – I fell down the doctor's trap in the Jardin des Tuileries and might have landed on her. I broke bottles too – there was so much fog, I thought she was a ghost. Sorry, Véronique!" cried Luc, but Véronique was already at the door of Pufont's Button Bijouterie. Before the crowd merged around them, Madame turned and pointed at Piaf.

"Tomorrow, ma petite plume," Madame yelled, "I am fixing your hair."

"Good idea," said Bertie with a smirk. "And *I* will fix this, Chestnut Roaster. You will have the best roaster in all of Paris!" He held up a wooden slat, then plucked a metal dish from between his legs. It was part of the brazier. "I can make it better than new, all of it!" He tipped a wooden box with his foot, once used beneath Piaf's feet to grant her some height at her roaster.

"I won't be needing that bit," said Piaf, pointing at the box. She felt tall enough as it was.

Bertie began assembling and fixing, there and then.

Luc walked over to the sinkhole and sat down, his legs dangling over its edge. His face was red, his fingers kneaded his thighs.

Piaf poked his shoulder.

"It's nothing," he said.

Piaf's face told him that wasn't enough.

"It's just that *nothing* can fix me. Not even Rapiditus's cure oil. I just wanted my memories back."

Luc twisted and pulled at his tight shirt until it ripped along the seams on one side. Piaf helped him rip the other side too.

"Better?"

He smiled and wiggled his toes. It was only then that Piaf noticed he had removed his too-tight shoes. He looked bedraggled and a bit like his twin. "Better."

Piaf cleared stones and debris away with her foot and sat down beside him.

She took a deep breath, put her squirrel button

into her pocket and stilled her fidgeting fingers. She allowed her mind to disappear down the deepest tunnels of her mind, right back to the very, very beginning. *Start somewhere.*

"All Fools' Day, twelve years ago," she began. "That was a wet Saturday, and that was the day we were born..."

THE END

In Actual Fact

Sometimes, when I walk down a bustling shopping street or a quiet country lane, I close my eyes and wish that, when I open them again, I will have travelled hundreds of years into the past. What would I see? Would the world smell differently? Could I walk in their shoes, manage a day's work, play the same games? And the birds – would they sing the same song back then?

It is no wonder that this curiosity led me to writing stories set in the past. Tantalising paintings and photographs helped me imagine long-lost worlds, and history books filled my mind with so many fascinating facts, even Luc would be impressed. So many *real* stories!

I then realised that, as a writer of stories of the

made-up kind, I had a power – an almost magical power. I could hold my pen like a paintbrush and add sparkle to those old paintings. I could take real historical facts and add a splash of wonder or mix a special tint for magic. If I chose wisely from my palette, it might be hard to separate fact from fiction.

Piaf's story is set in Paris in 1888. It might seem like a long time ago, but you need only go back about four generations – to the time of your great-great grandparents. It was at a time known in France as the 'Belle Époque' or 'beautiful era'. A time of elegance and optimism. To mark the 100th anniversary of the French Revolution, they would host the most spectacular World Fair – the *Exposition Universelle* of 1889. Paris, known as the *City of Lights* and world capital of fashion, was excited! Great minds of the world would marvel at the fair's mind-blowing exhibits, and visitors would feast their eyes on intriguing inventions. Even before arrival at the Exposition, they would be greeted by something extraordinary – something built especially for its grand entrance: *the Eiffel Tower*.

When I found a series of photographs showing the growing Eiffel Tower, I tried to imagine how the boutique owners, the busy street traders, the contemplating coffee-drinkers and the city's children felt on seeing such a spectacular giant rise slowly before their eyes. Indeed, a few dabs of my 'paintbrush' later and I wondered how they would react if they went to sleep one day in autumn 1888 and woke up forgetting the last year – to them, the tower would have grown from the first image in the below row of towers, to the fifth overnight!

NOV 1887 MAR 1888 JUN 1888 AUG 1888 DEC 1888 MAR 1889

I supposed the characters living in the real Paris of 1888 would be in awe of their new tower, but our history books tell a different tale. Like Piaf, not everyone was impressed by it. To many, the rising tower was a beast, and an ugly one at that, some describing it as 'obnoxious' and another describing it as a 'giant ungainly skeleton'. They settled for its

338

construction on the promise it would be dismantled within 20 years. Imagine! Paris sans Tour Eiffel!

Thankfully, its designer and technology had other plans. Gustave Eiffel installed a weather station on the third floor to enable cutting edge scientific experiments, and soon people realised the tower could be useful, even as a giant antenna for the latest invention – the radio. The tower was saved. Time-travel back to today, and the 1,000ft tall tower with its 1,065 steps and 20,000 lightbulbs welcomes millions of visitors each year and it is unarguably the most recognisable manmade monument in the world.

Paris is known for countless such landmarks and glorious treasures but, unlike the Eiffel Tower, not all survived. One lost treasure was the fantastical 13th Century *Grande Châsse* of Sainte-Chapelle. It was an enormous shrine made of silver and gilded bronze with no less than ten locks that could only be opened by royalty, and it was said to have cost even more than the glorious chapel in which it was placed! King Louis IX stored his most precious relics, or holy treasures, in the Grande Châsse – there were twenty-two in all, including the *Crown of Thorns* and a piece of the *True Cross*. It is thought by some that the rectangular chest as seen in the below image of the Grande Châsse (and where I boldly allowed the twins to hide!) might once have held one of the most precious relics of all – the infamous *Shroud of Turin* or *Holy Cloth*. Alas, we might never know, as one-hundred years before Piaf's time, during the French Revolution, the Grande Châsse was seen as an unwanted symbol of religion and royalty, so it was melted down. I wonder what Piaf and Luc would have thought had they found something precious in there while they played hide and seek with the grouchy knight?

In the absence of a Grande Châsse in which to hide, Paris has something else to offer – something remarkable: its underground maze of quarried caverns, secret chambers and squirming tunnels, some barely big enough to wriggle through. Paris is known for its architecture and these underground quarries were the birthplace of the stone used to create such buttery-yellow marvels as Notre-Dame. Though the existence of the underground city comes as some surprise to Piaf, the estimated nearly 200 miles of tunnels made their presence known throughout Parisian history. In the 1770s, a deadly sinkhole known as the 'Mouth of Hell' swallowed houses along one quarter of a mile at Rue d'Enfer. A few years on, the hidden chambers were used as burial sites during the French Revolution, and later, during World War II, the French Resistance fighters used the dark and deep tunnels as hideouts while other chambers were converted into bunkers by German soldiers. Secret parties and concerts were held underground, explorers explored, and artists left their mark with wild and wonderful murals. Of course, they were never alone for the ghost of poor Philibert Aspairt, a man said to have disappeared underground, is said to roam the darkest routes.

One small section, known as the *Catacombs*, is open to the public today, and it has some very strange inhabitants indeed – the bones of six million people! At the end of the 18th Century, Paris's cemeteries were overflowing. The streets held the stench of corpses, bones collapsed into neighbouring buildings. By cover of night, the corpses were carried by horse and black cloth-covered wagons to the Catacombs where workers fashioned impressive displays out of the bones themselves.

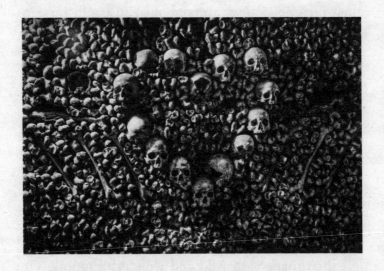

Beyond this small section, Paris's underground world remains closed to the public, for the greatest maze is a place of the greatest danger – if crumbling tunnels, sinkholes and flooded tunnels don't get you first, it is very likely you will get lost. That is, unless you have a memory like Piaf!

The workings of Piaf's extraordinary mind echo the Catacombs with its endless squirming tunnels and passageways. She imagined each memory was categorised and stored neatly in a wooden box in the tunnels of her mind and each box linked to countless other memories. Though these boxes were a figment of her (or my!) imagination, the ability to remember every life event in great detail is not – it is an ultra-rare condition (or superpower!) known as *Hyperthymesia*. The few people who live daily with the condition often need to find ways to distract themselves from disappearing into their past. In petite Piaf's case, that was to fidget and flutter – hence her name Piaf, meaning 'little sparrow'.

A Second Look

The Illustrations by
Ewa Beniak-Haremska

Piaf and her Paris

It is Paris 1888, the time of *Belle Époque* – a period of optimism and prosperity. The great Exposition Universelle is planned for the following year, and the new and rising Eiffel Tower will mark the entrance to the fair. Nestled amongst all that bustle, brilliance and beauty, is Piaf – a girl who cannot forget, even if she wanted to. Her name means 'little sparrow', and she was named this because she was as small as a bird when she was born.

Piaf on her Corner at

Rue du Dragon   Pages: 74–75

On her corner, where the quiet Rue du Dragon meets the bustling Boulevard Saint-Germain, petite Piaf stands at her chestnut roaster. A stranger arrives – can you spot him? Thankfully, Madame Legrand is nearby at Pufont's Button Bijouterie. As the chestnut burns and fog swirls thick as vanilla cream, a black cat signals a warning of what is to come.

From the Sinkhole to

the Asylum at Hôtel-Dieu   Pages: 76–77

From terrifying sinkholes beneath Rue du Dragon, to Luc's depressing room in Hôtel-Dieu's asylum. Which is worse, do you think? Piaf is haunted by images of twenty missing children, their pictures having appeared on *Le Petit Parisien* newspaper over the course of the past year. How many children can you see? Is **Véronique** – the girl with the crooked nose – there too?

Piaf & Luc rest in

Sainte-Chapelle   Pages: 142–143

The power of the chapel, made of so much glass

it renders its golden stone delicate, makes Piaf feel infinitely tiny and powerful all at once. Can you picture the colours bursting from that rose window? And amongst all that stained-glass, golden treasure and exquisite beauty, is the doctor. Do you see the four knights of the Order of the Holy Sepulchre?

A Miracle at Notre-Dame?   Pages: 144–145

Piaf and Luc are on the run! Posters declaring the twins *Wanted* are plastered to every surface and a carnival of people gather at the great cathedral of Notre-Dame. *A miracle!* the crowd roars. At first, Piaf wonders if the ugly stone gargoyles – each creature so petite, yet so fierce – and rows of statues are moving. If you stare long enough, perhaps they will.

**Tagine-Pot Hollow and
the Museum of Objects**   Pages: 232–233

One city, filled with boutiques, sparkling lights and life, the other, hidden, filthy, and ignored. So different and yet so alike. Piaf and Luc fall into Paris's underground twin where, amongst putrid dead mice, fingers of green slime, furry balls of fungus and skeletons of things long dead, lives Bertie, the best button maker in Paris. He spends his time carving in his Museum of Objects. What objects can you see? Madame Legrand's Russian dolls? A fox? How many roosters can you find? Be careful – the ghost of Philibert Aspairt might be there!

The Bone Well and
the Empire of the Dead Pages: 234–235
Using the leaf skeleton's map, Piaf leads Luc and Bertie through the Bone Well and on to the Empire of the Dead where skulls the colour of teeth glare down upon them and bones crunch and clop underfoot. They are on a mission, but are they alone?

Château Legrand, beneath
the Dôme des Invalides Pages: 332–333
Hooked by the scent of spices, Piaf crawls through a chatière – a narrow shaft – and arrives in Madame Legrand's secret underground home. All was still and it was silent, like a pharaoh's tomb deep inside one of the Egyptian pyramids. Everything about this place was Madame Legrand; rich fabrics, towers of spice, great rugs of terracotta and ochre and a stained-glass oil lamp, its steady flame splashing colour on every

surface. Somewhere, hidden deep inside, lies Empress Josephine. Where do you think it might be?

A Storm of Creatures
and the Apothecary

Pages: 334–335

They pelted at her shins, climbing higher and higher until they swirled and wrapped around her body, slapping her face and tangling her hair. *Creatures.* They nipped at her bare heels, she ran faster, they smacked off her hair, she ran faster screaming at the boys for help. Until, like a cat bored with its injured prey, the creatures stopped dead. She had arrived at the Apothecary where hundreds of tiny glass bottles all clinked in her wake. Were they tonics? Concoctions or tinctures? Or the stolen abilities of twenty gifted children?

Acknowledgements

It took time for the story of The Chestnut Roaster to evolve and so many kind people helped it grow into the book you hold in your hand today. When it was no more than a seed in my mind, my writing buddies, Olivia Hope, Susan Maxwell, Colin McArdle, Kevin Moran, Ciara O'Connor, Fran Quinn and Aisling White helped it sprout roots and gave me the courage to carry on – thank you! The tangle of words that would eventually become a first draft were hacked and pruned into shape by the brilliant and mega-patient E R Murray – huge thanks to the Words Ireland National Mentorship Programme and the Wexford County Council Arts Department for the opportunity to work with such an inspirational mentor.

To my editor, Mikka at Everything With Words, thank you for making this publishing journey so magical – I am so grateful for all your advice and support, and for giving me the opportunity to work once more with the incredible designer, Holly Ovenden – I truly adore the cover! And thank you for introducing me to the brilliant artist, Ewa Beniak-Haremska, whose internal illustrations stole my heart.

To all the wonderful book bloggers and booksellers out there who championed my debut book, Elsetime, especially the incredible team at Halfway Up The Stairs bookshop – you deserve all the sticky buns! To Juliette Saumande for inspiration en français – merci! Big love to Theresa Kelly and all the wonderful librarians and schoolteachers who brought me straight to my readers – I am in awe of the work you do.

I am so grateful for the encouragement of the amazingly talented Sinéad O'Hart and for the super-kind Time Tunnellers team of Susan Brownrigg, Catherine Randall, Barbara Henderson, Ally Sherrick and Jeannie Waudby who collectively splashed water on my face and told me to keep going – I can't thank you enough.

To Vanessa Fox O'Loughlin for your endless

support and advice, thank you so much. Big hugs, Niamh Garvey, Patricia Forde and the WonderFest team, how you keep me smiling! To our rock, the team at Children's Books Ireland, who kept children's writers and illustrators together through tricky times. And throughout it all, from seed to book, for your kindness and guidance, for the laughs and challenges, thank you Sarah Webb. Huge shoutout to our super-talented Writing Club gang – you are an inspiration!

To Moira, Dee and Rían, thank you for listening to my endless plot ramblings and writing woes.

To my biggest believer, Dad, this book is for you.

And finally, three little squeezes to my fellow chestnut hunters and wonderlarkers, Jerry, Bobby and Faye – hey, who knew we'd find a whole story hidden inside one of those chestnut burrs?

About the Author

Eve is a children's author and artist who lives in Co Wexford with her husband, twins, a dog and three cats. Having recognised the similarities between a blank canvas and a blank page, her writing career kicked off following a visit to a fortune-teller who told her to *Write! Write! Write!* Eve provides creative writing and crafting workshops to libraries, schools, writing clubs and festivals. Find out more about Eve and her books on www.evemcdonnell.com, or say hello via Twitter or Instagram @Eve_Mc_Donnell.

About the Illustrator

Ewa is a Polish artist living in Warsaw. Her works have been exhibited in galleries in Poland and abroad, mainly in Rome, where she studied drawing and painting. She has illustrated several dozen books for children. Some of them received significant awards and distinctions. While illustrating books she travels. She gets to know the mind and soul of the writer which in turn enriches her world view. In recent years, she usually chooses drawing, which allows her to respond intuitively and is limited to simple tools. Her work is very lyrical and has a strong touch of magical realism. She likes silence and precise, demanding craft work. She looks at the world from afar.